MW01143204

Perfect Blue

Laura Langston

Fitzhenry & Whiteside

Copyright © 2002 by Laura Langston
First published as *A Taste of Perfection* by Stoddart Kids in 2002

Published in Canada by Fitzhenry & Whiteside,
195 Allstate Parkway, Markham, Ontario L3R 4T8

Published in the United States by Fitzhenry & Whiteside,
311 Washington Street, Brighton, Massachusetts 02135

All rights reserved. No part of this book may be reproduced in any manner
without the express written consent of the publisher, except in the case of brief
excerpts in critical reviews and articles. All inquiries should be addressed to
Fitzhenry & Whiteside Limited, 195 Allstate Parkway, Markham, Ontario L3R 4T8

www.fitzhenry.ca   godwit@fitzhenry.ca

10 9 8 7 6 5 4 3 2 1

Library and Archives Canada Cataloguing in Publication

Langston, Laura, 1958-
[Taste of perfection]
Perfect Blue / Laura Langston.
Previously published under title: A taste of perfection.
Toronto : Stoddart Kids, 2002.
ISBN 978-1-55455-058-6
1. Labrador retriever—Juvenile fiction. I. Title. II. Title: Taste of perfection.
PS8573.A5832T37 2008   jC813'.54   C2007-907006-X

**U.S. Publisher Cataloging-in-Publication Data
(Library of Congress Standards)**

Laura Langston
Perfect Blue / Laura Langston.
[240] p. : cm.
Summary: Mr. Lavender Blue is the perfect dog, and training him for the
show ring is the perfect opportunity for twelve-year-old Erin Morris to show
that she's responsible enough to have a dog of her own.
ISBN 978-1-55455-058-6
1. Science fiction. I. Title.
[Fic] dc22   PZ7.L2698Per 2008

Fitzhenry & Whiteside acknowledges with thanks the Canada Council for the
Arts, and the Ontario Arts Council for their support of our publishing program.
We acknowledge the financial support of the Government of Canada through
the Book Publishing Industry Development Program (BPIDP) for our publishing activities.

 Canada Council Conseil des Arts
for the Arts du Canada

Design by Fortunato Design Inc.
Cover image by Peter Hudecki

Printed in Canada

Acknowledgments

Thanks to Dr. John Ennals for his veterinary
insights, and to Chelsea, Lauren,
and Judy Birmingham for their invaluable
comments on dog shows.

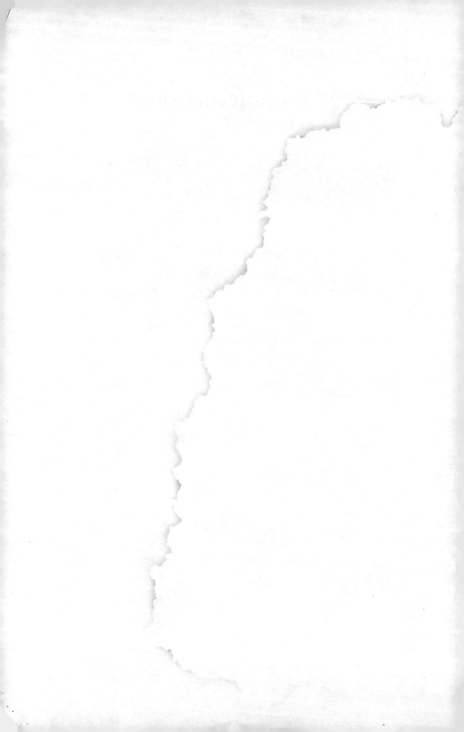

Chapter One

SOMETIMES ERIN MORRIS tasted things no one else could taste. And today she tasted bliss.

It fizzed and popped in her mouth, exploding into tastes like triple brownie sundaes, double cheese pizza, and nacho buttered popcorn. Bliss was an I'm-going-to-burst-if-I-don't-tell-someone kind of flavor, and Erin couldn't wait to get home and share the news with her mom and dad.

"Can you believe I was picked to work at the SPCA this summer?" Fingering the slip of pink paper she'd tucked between her books, Erin glanced at Rachel. "Now my parents will have to get me a dog." The spring sun hit her square in the face as she walked home from Ridgeway Elementary School with her best friend.

Erin's face was stuck in smile mode. Even her pile of homework didn't bother her. Even the second wart she'd discovered on the third knuckle of her left hand didn't bother her. Dogs and cats didn't worry about warts. Why should she?

"The Society for the Prevention of Cruelty to Animals." She tested the words on her tongue. They sounded wonderful. "The SPCA."

"Um hm." Rachel was clearly getting tired of the conversation.

"I know it's volunteer and three other kids were picked too, but this is my chance. My parents want me to be responsible and show I can handle animals. This is perfect!"

"Right." Rachel didn't even look at Erin. She stared down Moody Avenue to Keith Road where three boys rollerbladed. "Too bad it doesn't pay," she said sympathetically.

Erin didn't care. She was happy to volunteer two afternoons a week at the North Vancouver facility. Thrilled, in fact. "When Mr. Parker called me down to the office along with those other kids, I couldn't figure out what I'd done." Erin knew she was babbling but she couldn't help it. It was the first time in her life she'd tasted bliss and it was making her tongue crazy. "I couldn't believe it when he told me my essay had gotten me one of the four volunteer positions."

But Rachel wasn't really listening. "Mmm hmm." They turned the corner on Keith Road where a gang of kids gathered outside Winson's Market. "Look," she said brightly, "there are the Oresti twins!" She smoothed her long, blonde hair and walked faster. "Come on, hurry up."

Erin tucked the pink slip back between her books and automatically slipped her left hand into the pocket of her jeans.

"Aren't they the cutest?" Rachel giggled nervously as the two girls walked through the crowd, past pots of bright red flowers and buckets of yellow daffodils to the Oresti twins.

Cute wasn't the word Erin would use to describe Anthony and Joseph Oresti. Especially not with their mouths full of barbecue chips. They looked like overstuffed teddy bears dressed in blue jeans and gray T-shirts. Erin giggled. Even their dog, Patches, had traces of brown barbecue powder around his white muzzle.

"Hi, guys!" Rachel stopped. "What math pages are we supposed to do, anyway?"

Erin rolled her eyes. Rachel just wanted a reason to talk to the twins. Her best friend had discovered boys last year, and every few months she had a crush on someone new. For a while Rachel had even been crazy about Erin's neighbor Bruce.

Joseph Oresti pulled out his math book and Rachel leaned close. Erin sighed to herself. Boys were okay—if they had something interesting to say and if she didn't have.to look down at them. But most of the ones she knew mumbled a lot and were almost a head shorter than she was. Not only that, most of them were dumb enough to fall for that line about homework. Erin bent down to give Patches a scratch on his head.

Poor Patches. The dog smelled bad and he was ugly. His brown coat had fallen out in chunks, leaving patches of red, blistered skin. Erin didn't know if that was why he was called Patches or if it was because he wore a red patch over his left eye. Apparently he'd lost the eye years ago in a fight with a raccoon.

Rachel laughed at something Anthony said, and the two boys started play punching each other. Erin gave Patches one final scratch behind the ear and stood up. "Come on, Rachel," she urged impatiently. "Let's go."

"Hey!" A shrill whistle broke out behind them. The fizz in Erin's mouth dissolved. Her stomach sank. She knew that voice. "The crowd's all here. Let's party!" The other kids stopped talking. Joseph and Anthony stopped punching each other and looked warily at the newcomer. Slowly Erin and Rachel turned.

Deryk Latham. In a black leather jacket and faded black jeans. Sitting on his mountain bike. "Hey, Beauty." His washed-out blue eyes lingered on Rachel before they flicked to Erin. "Hey, Beast." He grinned.

Laughter rippled through the crowd. Erin's face flamed. Beauty and the Beast. That's what they called her and Rachel this year. And Deryk Latham had started it.

Erin looked down at Rachel. Her straight blonde hair never frizzed. Her skin was clear and her teeth were straight. Her jeans were perfectly faded, even her white T-shirt was spotlessly clean. Everything about Rachel was perfect. Sometimes Erin secretly wished her friend would get a really big pimple on the end of her nose. Then she'd feel guilty for thinking it.

"Don't be such a creep, Latham." Rachel stood up for Erin like she always did.

Deryk Latham turned to the Oresti twins. "And then there's Pork and Chop," he drawled. "With their dog, Stink."

The ripples of laughter turned into hoots and hollers. "Pork and Chop and their dog, Stink," jeered a skinny boy with red hair. The crowd began to chant. "Stink, Stink, and their dog, Stink."

Joseph's face turned pink. "Come on," he said to Anthony, "let's go!" He grabbed Patches's collar and pulled. Patches dug in his heels and refused to move. The crowd hooted again.

"Go, Stink, go!" another boy taunted.

Deryk Latham smirked. Beside her Rachel giggled. "Patches really is ugly," she whispered loudly.

Erin fumed as she watched Joseph tug on the dog. Dogs probably didn't get embarrassed. Not like she did when the kids teased her about being too tall, or tripping over her feet, or all the other things they teased her about. But Patches didn't deserve to be dragged around—even if he was ugly.

"Don't be mean to him," Erin said loudly.

"Sure, Beast, sure!" Deryk Latham lifted the front wheel of his bike and spun it forward.

The movement captivated Patches, who broke free from Joseph and waddled over to the bike.

"Go, Stink, go!" the boy with the red hair chanted again.

And the dog did.

Patches lifted his leg and peed all over Deryk Latham's back tire. He stood for a minute and stared at Deryk before waddling back to the Oresti twins.

The crowd howled with laughter. Even Erin laughed. That was one way to stand up for yourself!

"Hey, you filthy, stinkin' dog," Deryk Latham snarled. His blue eyes darkened as he stared at Patches.

"A first-class Stink job," someone yelled.

"Go, Stink, go!" someone added.

"Come on." Anthony looked nervously at Deryk Latham. "We'd better get out of here."

"Clear out, clear out!" Mr. Flores walked out of Winson's Market and stood under the red and blue Lotto 649 sign. His arms were loaded with the magazines he'd been shelving. "You buy your food and you leave." His black eyebrows were drawn angrily across his forehead. "No loitering or I'll call the police."

Deryk Latham left first. With another angry glance at the Oresti twins and Patches, he flipped on his helmet and pushed off.

Erin and Rachel headed in the opposite direction. "Latham is such a creep saying all those things about you and the twins," Rachel said sympathetically.

"He's a creep, period." Erin hated being teased but at least she had loyal friends like Rachel, who didn't care if she was tall or clumsy. "Patches sure showed Deryk Latham," she said with a giggle.

Rachel wrinkled her nose and grinned. "I'll bet he spends two hours washing that bike!" She glanced back to the Oresti twins, who were following slowly behind. "I don't know why you want to work with dogs all summer. Camp's going to be way cooler...and you'll have to miss it." Rachel lowered her voice. "At least the twins will be there. I just hope they don't bring that stinky Patches."

"They shouldn't be so mean to him," Erin repeated. If Patches were her dog, she'd bathe him and love him and keep him away from Deryk Latham.

Turning the corner onto her street, Erin saw her dad's car. They were over a block from home, but the bright yellow Mazda was hard to miss. "That's weird," she murmured with a frown. Erin couldn't remember the last time her dad had come home in the afternoon. Maybe a few days before Christmas. But never in mid-June.

"Weird? What's weird?" But Rachel didn't wait for Erin's answer. Instead she tossed her head over her shoulder and giggled as she caught one last glimpse of the Oresti twins pulling Patches down the road. When they disappeared around the corner, she turned back to Erin. "I still think Anthony is cuter than Joseph, don't you?" When Erin didn't answer, Rachel asked again, "What's weird?"

"Dad's home," Erin replied. "Early." A dog barked in the distance and Erin remembered the pink slip of paper she'd tucked between her two books. The fizz was back in her mouth. She couldn't wait to get home and tell him the good news.

"Are you sure you can't come to camp *and* work at the SPCA?" Rachel asked.

"No way!" Erin shook her head and began to walk faster. "I said I'd be available for the whole summer and I'm going to be." If her parents agreed. Of course they would. They wanted her to learn responsibility, didn't they?

"I wouldn't want to spend two afternoons a week with a bunch of smelly dogs."

But Erin wasn't listening. Her mother's blue SUV was in the driveway, too. Weird. Her mother was teaching today. She'd left before Erin had finished breakfast. What was going on?

Suddenly Erin knew.

Her parents were cooking up a wonderful surprise. Twice that Erin could remember her parents had whisked her away on a mini holiday. Once, they'd gone to see a rodeo. Another time they'd traveled to Washington State to see the tulip festival. Erin's imagination kicked into overdrive. Maybe it was a bigger surprise this time. Like leaving tonight for a week at Disneyland. Her parents had been promising that for years.

Well, she had a surprise of her own!

Rachel stopped in front of Erin's house and gestured to the yellow Mazda. "That's still the coolest car I've ever seen."

"Dad says it takes corners perfectly. I don't know about that but it sure goes on the highway." Erin glanced at the house. The front curtains were closed. Maybe they'd bought a new TV—one of those huge fifty-eight-inch plasma things!

"They finally finished painting, huh?" Rachel's eyes were glued to the next door neighbor's house and Bruce's bedroom window.

Erin nodded and tried hard not to smile. In spite of her crush on the Oresti twins, Rachel still liked Bruce.

"It looks good." Rachel pretended to look at the new paint on the house but Erin knew she was still looking for the basketball star, who was two years ahead of them in school.

"I've gotta go," Erin said.

Rachel pulled her eyes from Bruce's bedroom window. "And tell them your news, right?"

Erin nodded. "See you tomorrow, Rachel."

Erin's steps slowed as she reached the front door. She wanted to stretch out the excitement, like she stretched out the presents at Christmas.

Murmured voices came from the kitchen as she

closed the front door. Quickly she poked her head into the living room. No new TV. No travel brochures on the coffee table. She pulled the pink slip from the two books and waved it in the air as she walked into the kitchen.

"Hi." She dumped her books on the counter and gave her parents a grin. "You'll never believe what happened to me today!"

There were no answering smiles, no encouraging words. Just two pairs of eyes staring at her. And the smell of stale coffee hanging in the air. She scanned the kitchen table. It was littered with papers and envelopes and a few bills. No plane tickets. At least none she could see. "You'll never believe it," she repeated, her grin slipping just a little.

There was silence. Silence and a strange, flat look in her father's brown eyes. Sadness. Erin couldn't remember the last time her father had been sad. He was always joking, laughing. She glanced at her mother but couldn't see her eyes. Mom was staring into her coffee cup.

"What's wrong?"

Her father's lips tightened.

Something was wrong.

"Sit down." Dad reached for a chair and pulled it out. "We have something to tell you."

15

Her legs folded like two limp strands of spaghetti. She sat. Slowly her mother raised her head. Her blue eyes were rimmed in red. She'd been crying. Erin's stomach lurched.

"Is it...is it...?" She tried to whisper around the lump in her throat but the words got stuck. "Is it Grandma?"

"Grandma's fine, sweetheart." Mom reached out and tucked a loose strand of Erin's hair behind her ear. She attempted a smile but it only reached half her mouth. "Your dad's lost his job, Erin. He's been forced to take early retirement."

"Retirement?" She frowned. "That's for—"

"Old people?" Her father interrupted gently. His face wrinkled into a sad grin and his eyes lost some of their strange flatness. "I'm fifty-one, Erin. Not so young anymore."

Her father wasn't old. Old people didn't jog or cycle around the Gulf Islands. Old people didn't shoot baskets and drive cool yellow cars.

"You're not old," she told him hotly. "You're the perfect age." She looked at her mother, sure she would agree, but her mother was silent. "Besides, you've been an accountant with Landers and Berg practically forever. They can't make you retire. They can't make you do anything," she said fiercely. "People have free will. You're always telling me that."

Her father nodded. "You're right; they can't make me do anything. But the company is in trouble." He tapped his fingers on the table. "They've given me two choices. Take early retirement or be laid off. Maybe even fired."

"Fired?" Her heart began to pound. "But that's illegal. We learned about that in Social Studies. They can't fire you without…without—"

"Cause," her mother said softly. "They can't fire your father without cause." Mom smiled and this time it worked. It was one of those "brave" smiles, the kind she reserved for trips to the dentist.

"Right," Erin whispered. There was a pit of gloom in her stomach. She wanted to tell her parents about the job at the SPCA, but it wouldn't be the same. Not now. "Without cause," she repeated.

"They have cause," Dad explained. "They're in financial trouble. If they don't let fifteen people go, they'll have to shut the doors completely."

"We'll manage." Mom pushed her coffee away and turned in her seat to face Erin. "We'll tighten up, watch the spending. I'm going to teach summer school again this year. Your father will look for another job. There's no law against that." She hesitated. "But I'm afraid we'll have to cancel your summer camp with Rachel. Maybe even see if we can get the deposit back."

"Okay." Erin nodded slowly. Her father out of work? It seemed so weird. "I have good news," she finally offered shyly.

"Right!" her father said with forced cheerfulness. "You said something happened today."

In spite of the gloom in her stomach, she grinned. "I'm going to be volunteering at the SPCA two afternoons a week this summer." The words tumbled out so fast her parents had no time to speak, no time to congratulate her. "You know how you've always told me to prove I could be responsible for a dog. Well, I did—I mean I will! I entered this contest and four winners were picked. I was one of them," she said proudly. "So I don't care about summer camp because I won't have time to go."

Her parents exchanged looks.

"I know it's not a paying job or anything," Erin rushed on, "but Mr. Richards said if you're good and you volunteer long enough, sometimes you get hired on. And once you prove yourself, they'll even let you adopt a stray!" She waved the pink slip in the air. "All you have to do is sign this consent form and I'll be a full-fledged volunteer."

Her parents exchanged second looks. Mom's eyes filled with tears again.

"What?" The gloom was back, swimming in her stomach like an angry shark. "What is it?"

"What your mother's trying to say is that this summer is not…" Her father stopped.

She could feel the gloom shark snapping at her happiness.

"Not what?" she asked nervously.

"Not the summer for the SPCA," her mother said gently. "I'm going back up north to teach at Camp Belvedere for six weeks this summer. Your dad's been under a huge amount of pressure over the last few months, so he's coming with me to unwind and think about his future."

Camp Belvedere was all healthy, all natural. All disgusting. Mom loved it. Erin hated it. She'd survived one week there last summer. One week of cold showers, unheated cabins, and so much healthy food she was practically green by the time she left. There wasn't a chocolate bar or potato chip allowed within a thousand miles of the place.

"I don't want to go back there," she said.

"I figured that," Mom said. "So you'll be spending the summer with Grandma."

Chapter Two

ERIN STRETCHED HER HAND OUT the SUV window and let the wind rush through her fingers. The July sun was hot; the shoelace-shaped clouds trailing through the sky offered no relief. It would have helped if she'd worn shorts instead of capris. And if her father hadn't sold the yellow Mazda. Then they'd be traveling to Courtenay with the top off and the wind ripping the knots out of her hair. But the car was gone and everything had changed.

Everything!

Instead of working at the SPCA all summer, Erin was spending seven weeks with her grandmother in Courtenay. She loved her grandma, and she loved spending time with her, but helping Grandma was like helping out around the house. The SPCA would have meant taking direction from other adults, dealing with the public, looking after sick animals. It would have meant real responsibility.

"I think parking gets worse in Nanaimo every

month," Dad grumbled as he circled the block again and pulled up in front of the Nanaimo Bakery. Stopping at the bakery before hitting the highway for the one-hour drive to Courtenay was one of their summer rituals.

"How about running in and buying a dozen of those sticky buns Grandma likes, Erin?" Mom reached into her wallet and handed her a ten-dollar bill. "Get me a muffin and you and Dad Danishes or something, okay? We'll circle the block a few times."

"Fine." Erin took the money, jumped out of the car, and slammed the door behind her. Her parents were trying so hard to be nice but she didn't care. She didn't even care that her father had phoned the SPCA and tried to fix things. There might be a volunteer spot for Erin in the fall, they'd said. But there were no guarantees.

There was a tiny stair at the edge of the doorway but Erin didn't see it. Her foot caught. She tripped. An older man eating a jelly doughnut gave her a sympathetic smile; Erin pretended not to notice. She'd be glad when her feet stopped growing.

The bakery was packed. Young parents were buying loaves of bread and popular chocolate treats for toddlers in strollers. Businesspeople in the small café were talking over coffee and brioche. Young people were stocking up on pizza bread and sausage rolls for an afternoon at the beach. Erin lined up behind three girls carrying backpacks and wearing bikini tops and cutoffs. One of the girls glanced at Erin before turning back to her friends. Tall, blonde, and wearing black Vuarnet sunglasses, she reminded Erin slightly of Rachel.

The line moved quickly. "Next," called a plump woman with a frazzled look on her face. Erin placed her order and waited. The woman returned with a bag and Erin reached for it.

The girl with the Vuarnet glasses reached for it, too. "I think that's mine."

Erin backed off. "Oh, sorry."

"Don't touch her hand, Sue," said one of the other girls as she played with a silver ring on her finger. "You might end up with warts, too."

Erin pretended not to hear but there was a hot, bitter taste in her mouth. She watched the girl named Sue check her bag.

"I could live with the warts," whispered a third girl with a purple streak in her brown hair. "But talk about revolting legs."

Six inches showing beneath her capris and she was still getting razzed, Erin thought.

"Hasn't she seen the inside of a tanning bed?" the

voice continued. "Or heard of razors?" Wanting to drown out their whispers, Erin counted the specialty chocolates displayed on a nearby tray. Ten baseballs, six tennis rackets, thirteen cats, and six hedgehogs.

"Come on, guys." Satisfied that she had the right order, the girl named Sue turned to go. "She can't help her legs or her warts. Any more than she can help being so tall."

Their laughter echoed in Erin's ears long after they left the bakery. Finally, after she had counted chocolates twice and was starting to count the bread, the clerk with the frazzled look returned. Erin accepted the order, grabbed her change, and bolted for the door, being extra careful to step over the stair.

Her parents weren't there. The three girls were.

Erin looked down the street and willed her parents to hurry up. She pretended not to notice the girls eyeing her. She pretended not to hear them.

Where *were* they? Without the Mazda, her father was driving like an old man.

The girl with the purple streak in her hair giggled. "I used to think you got warts from touching frogs but warts are just a virus like a cold, only uglier."

"Too bad she has so many colds." They laughed.

Erin took a deep breath, turned her head, and

stared at them. The girl named Sue looked embarrassed and elbowed the others. They quickly shut up. Erin decided Sue wasn't as pretty as Rachel after all. She also decided the girl with the silver ring had squinty eyes and the one with the purple streak in her hair had a neck like a giraffe. That made her feel better.

When Erin saw the familiar SUV and the welcoming faces of her mother and father, she jumped into the car and slammed the door behind her.

She handed her mother the change. "I got Grandma's sticky buns, Danishes for me and Dad, and one of those healthy muffins with dried apricots and flax and stuff for you." She resisted the urge to stick out her tongue at the three girls standing on the corner. Instead, she turned her back on them as her father pulled away from the curb.

Erin had planned to finish her Danish before she asked her mother the question but she couldn't wait. "Mom?"

"Mmm hmm?" Her mother was taking slow bites out of her muffin. She always ate slowly when she really liked something.

"Can I please get a tan?"

"You know my position, Erin. Tanning causes cancer. I packed you five bottles of sunscreen and I expect you to use it every day. Why are you bringing this up again?"

Because a tan would hide the warts on her hands and make her skinny legs look way better. "Because everybody else gets tanned." Everybody but her mother, who practically bathed in some natural sunscreen product she bought at the health food store.

"I'm sorry, Erin." Mom popped a corner of her muffin into her mouth.

"Not even a light one?" Erin wheedled. "Just on my hands and legs? To...you know..." *Hide my imperfections.* "To make them look better."

"Oh, Erin." Her mother sighed. "Is this about the warts and hair?" She didn't wait for an answer. "You can shave or wax your legs any time you want. And I'm sure the sassafras oil will work on your warts eventually. Remember what the doctor said? We don't want to take a chance with those harsh chemicals."

"But the warts are ugly." Erin bit into the blueberry center of her Danish. The warts on her left hand stared up at her. Her "crater claw," Deryk Latham called it. "And that doctor isn't a real doctor."

"Dr. Roth is a registered naturopath." Mom's let's-be-reasonable voice had turned into her no-nonsense one. "And like she said, they'll probably disappear eventually. If not, we'll look at getting them burned off next year."

Next year? She could be one giant, hairy, white-skinned wart by then.

"Natural is best, remember?"

"Natural is gross." Erin grumbled. Bits of blueberry Danish flew across the backseat. Her mother was anti-tanning, anti-chemicals. She wouldn't wear makeup. Even her shampoo was some gross brown stuff from the health food store.

"Dad?" Erin pleaded. "Mom's being unreasonable."

Her dad stepped on the gas. Finally they were through the Nanaimo traffic and on the highway to Courtenay. "This is your mother's department, Erin. Not mine." Dad didn't care about being natural. He used ordinary shampoo, regular toothpaste, and when he was sick, he bought over-the-counter medicines. But when Erin was sick, he made sure she got regular medicine even though Mom insisted on giving her herbs too. Unfortunately, Dad left the makeup and grooming issues up to Mom. "But as far as I'm concerned, bug-face," he added. "You're perfect the way you are."

The familiar phrase usually made Erin smile. Not today. "Perfectly ugly," she muttered. With a crater claw and ugly legs and feet so big she tripped over them all the time.

Her mother turned to study her. "Erin, darling, we love you very much. I know it must seem unfair but I'm making these rules for your own good. I want you to be as healthy as you can be."

"A little bit of sun wouldn't kill me."

"Remember what I told you?" Mom finished her muffin, wiped her fingers on a tissue. "Hundreds of years ago, a tan was something to be ashamed of. It was a sign of being lower class. Nowadays, people are starting to realize tanning is bad for you. In the not-too-distant future, having tanned skin will be the sign of a very bad choice. I like to think that you're on the cutting edge of a new trend."

"Great. So put me in a coma and wake me up in a hundred years when I'm in style."

Her father snort-laughed; her mother glared at him as she turned around.

The remainder of the trip was quiet. Erin tried to forget about the girls at the bakery. Instead, she thought about the SPCA. Today would have been her afternoon to work. She would have done such a good job, too. And by September she would have had a dog. No problemo.

Now she had no dog and no job. Instead, she had

ugly legs and crater claws and a mother who was so afraid of chemicals she even insisted on natural deodorant! Just what every girl needed.

Rachel was already at summer camp, probably giggling with the stupid Oresti twins. Erin could see it now.

The twins were standing by the lake, wearing bright orange bathing trunks. Their cheeks were stuffed with barbecue chips but they kept eating and eating. Faster and faster. Rachel stood beside them, in her new red bathing suit, staring up at them in perfect adoration. All of a sudden, the twins began punching each other. Bits of chomped and chewed barbecue chips began to fly. A huge wad landed in Rachel's hair. She screamed. Then a bee buzzed in for the kill.

"Erin. Earth to Erin." Dad broke into her daydream. "We're almost there."

They drove through downtown Courtenay and turned left just before the Puntledge River. The city soon gave way to thickets of trees and rolling fields. A few minutes later Erin saw a large white sign with its bouquet of flowers painted between two stenciled horses. It said Three Kilometers To The Walker

Farm. That's where Cassie lived. From there, it was just five minutes down the road to her grandmother's property.

"There's Cassie's sign." Mom pointed like she had every year since Erin was six. "You'll be glad to see Cassie again, won't you?"

"I'd rather be working at the SPCA and getting a dog than spending my whole entire summer in the middle of nowhere."

"That's enough," Dad warned.

Mom ignored her words. "I'll leave you some extra money so you and Grandma can go shopping," she said brightly.

Yuk. Her mother loved shopping. Erin didn't.

The road narrowed in front of them; the SUV dipped down the hill and turned sharply at the familiar bend. Stretching as far as the eye could see were fields of green, dotted with the yellow and pink flowers of early summer. It was Cassie's place, the Walker farm. Cassie's dad was a horse breeder. Her mother grew dried flowers for market.

Across the field was the red barn and familiar gray farmhouse. Was Cassie there waiting for her? In spite of her unhappiness, she felt a rush of excitement. Cassie was her summertime friend. She wasn't like Rachel at all. She wasn't interested in boys or clothes. She hated shopping, too. She wouldn't care about Erin's warts or the hair on her legs. All Cassie cared about was horses. And practical jokes, of course.

Erin grinned, remembering last year and how they'd put raspberry Jell-O in the toes of Mrs. Walker's garden clogs. They had scattered a couple of earthworms on the outside of the shoes first, then watched from their hiding spot as Mrs. Walker had picked them off. They'd managed to contain their laughter when Cassie's mom had slipped her bare feet into the green clogs and let out a wild screech, and they had avoided punishment by offering to clean out the fridge and freezer. Even that had been planned. They got to eat the last bits of ice cream from four different cartons. Yes, Erin thought, she couldn't wait to see Cassie again.

"Grandma's dogs will look so different," her mother was saying from the front seat. "Remember that Christmas card? I'm sure they've grown. What was Grandma talking about on the phone the other day? About Blue and Duchess and a surprise?"

A quiver of excitement rippled through Erin when she remembered her grandmother's voice on the other end of the phone. Grandma had something cooked up.

"Frankly, I'm amazed she's stuck with this dog thing," Dad said dryly. "I figured she'd be onto something else by now!"

"Steve!" Mom shook her head but a small smile turned the corner of her lips. "I always said your mother would find her niche one day."

Erin had grown up hearing all about Grandma Morris's niche. A niche, she had discovered, was like finding a special thing to do. Her grandmother was always trying new things. She wasn't like Rachel's grandmother, who knit socks and liked to cook. Grandma Morris was too busy to cook. For a while she'd taught yoga and then she'd gotten involved with a distance swimming club. She had been a tour bus operator and a home decorating consultant, and she had worked in so many offices Erin had lost count. Four years ago she had decided to breed dogs, something she had been interested in for a long time. Flat-Coat and Labrador Retrievers. As far as Erin was concerned, it was the best niche of all.

When the SUV slowed at the dented red mailbox and the familiar Dove Creek Kennels sign, Erin felt a rush of excitement. The whole summer was way too long but she still couldn't wait to see her grandmother. And Blue. And eat the strawberry shortcake Grandma always bought for her.

"Have to trim the holly again," her father said as the wagon made its way through the prickly green arch of bushes and up the gravel drive to the old stone house.

Her father said the same thing every year and every year she said the same thing back. "No, Dad. I like it bushy."

"Your grandmother and I don't." He tapped the brakes and brought the car to a stop.

Erin flicked her seat belt open and pulled on the car door. Even if he was out of a job, he was still the same old dad, always wanting things to be perfect. She could understand that. She wanted things to be perfect, too.

"Darlin', you made it!" The voice came from somewhere off to the right. But before Erin could open her mouth to answer, a large black ball of fur hurled itself at her chest and knocked her off her feet.

Chapter Three

"BLUE!" ERIN GASPED. A large, pink tongue slobbered over her face and across her eyes. She wrapped her arms around the sturdy black neck and squeezed. He was bigger than last year. "Hello, Blue, my Lavender Blue." The dog shook with excitement. His tongue frantically gave her a bath, traveling through her hair and around the back of her neck.

Erin tried to pull away but Blue wouldn't let her. "He remembers me." She giggled as Blue's tongue tickled the inside of her ear.

"O'course he does!" Erin's grandmother hurried down the walk—a tanned, smiling figure dressed in blue jeans and a vivid orange T-shirt. "Down, Blue. Down! That's enough, boy. Come here now." Firm hands pulled on the dog's collar and the Retriever had no choice but to come away from Erin. "Are you all right, darlin'?" Peggy Morris pulled Erin to her feet.

"I'm fine, Grandma." Blue sat reluctantly beside

his mistress, not taking his large eyes away from Erin and whimpering all the while.

"Well, look at you!" Grandma exclaimed with a smile. "You've grown taller." She gave Erin a hard hug with her one free arm.

"Too tall." She tucked her left hand into the pocket of her shorts and slouched forward slightly as she smiled into her grandmother's soft brown eyes.

"Not too tall at all, bug-face." Her father came up and gave her a gentle nudge. "No slouching now."

She stared at the ground. She was tired of her father calling her bug-face like he'd been doing forever. Blue whined again. His tail was wagging back and forth like a flag in the wind. He wanted to come back to her.

"Now, Steve, leave her be. She's perfect as she is." Grandma winked happily. Erin grinned.

"Peggy's right." Mom was always the last out of the car and today was no exception. "Besides, I slouched at her age and I grew out of it." She handed Grandma a parcel. "Hello, Peg. We brought you some of those sticky buns from the Nanaimo bakery."

"Wonderful!" Grandma released her grip on Blue, and Erin watched the two women hug. Her mother was small and blonde. Dainty. Delicate. Petite. Like Rachel. All those things Erin wanted to be but wasn't. She took after her father and her grandmother. The

Irish side of the family. Tall with pale skin and dark hair. Hair dark enough to get lost in, her grandmother always used to say. At least she said that back when *she* had dark hair. It had turned gray a few years ago and now Grandma dyed it. This year it was reddish brown. The color leaves turned in fall. Maybe she should dye her hair too. Or put in a few streaks. Something to raise her out of geekdom.

Mom would never go for it.

"The strawberry shortcake's waiting for you." Grandma wrapped an arm around Erin's shoulder. "Let's put away your things and then we can eat." They began to walk and as soon as they did, the black Retriever ran in circles around them, constantly whining and jumping.

"You've got yourself a fan there, Erin." Her dad grinned at the dog's antics. Just then a robin flew across the grass. Blue forgot all about Erin and ran after the bird.

"He's outgrowing his playfulness some, but he's still a handful." Grandma stared after the dog, a proud look on her face. "Always chasing after something." She gave Erin's shoulders a squeeze and started walking again. "Good potential, but he's still high-spirited."

The hedge of lavender lining the driveway was in

full bloom. Erin smelled the perfumed flowers as her legs brushed up against the skinny purple stalks. After realizing the bird was gone, Blue quickly rejoined them. He nudged Erin with the cold tip of his black nose. At the same time his feathery tail swished the bushes and sent a few tiny purple flecks into his fur.

"Still love the lavender, don't you, Blue?" She brushed the lavender blossoms away and hugged him. He licked her cheek and then stayed by her side as they went up the porch into the house.

Erin would never forget that Sunday morning two years ago when her grandmother had taken the puppies out to the front lawn. Blue had wandered away and she had found him sniffing the lavender bushes. His soft black fur had been covered with tiny purple-blue blossoms. From that moment, he had been 'Mr. Lavender Blue.' Blue for short.

"Toss your suitcase in the bedroom," Grandma instructed from the small kitchen off the hallway, "and come to the table. Blue, you go to your blanket now. We're going to eat."

"It's okay, Grandma. He can come with me." She rubbed Blue's head. She'd almost forgotten how wonderful his fur felt.

"While you put your things away then," her

grandmother smiled. "But Blue goes to his blanket while we eat. House rule."

Her grandmother didn't have many rules for people, but she had lots for her dogs. Last year, when she had come for a visit, Blue had been kenneled outside at night with the other animals. Erin had begged and pleaded to have him inside with her, just for the summer. Just for the summer had turned into forever, and now Blue occupied a place of honor in her grandmother's house. But he still had to follow her rules.

Grandma had one of Erin's favorites for lunch: grilled cheese sandwiches. She concentrated on her sandwich while the adults discussed her father's job options. Blue stayed quietly on his blanket by the stove, his head down, his eyes studying the four of them. If only she could have a dog like Blue, Erin thought as she studied him. If only!

"Blue's behavior is impeccable," her father commented later when they were eating dessert. "He hasn't moved an inch during lunch."

"I've been working on him," Grandma admitted with a slight smile. "He gets carried away sometimes, but he's the best dog I've ever produced. A real winner." Her smile deepened. "Meets the standard of perfection for his breed to a T." She studied Blue for a minute before continuing. "He had that special something when he was born, but I wasn't sure if he'd be show material. You know what I mean. Some dogs just have to grow into themselves."

"Like people," Mom added as she munched on a strawberry. As she did every year, she said no to the cake and cream and had fresh berries instead.

"Exactly!" Grandma stood and gathered dishes.

"How's the training going?" Dad asked.

"Very well. I spend twenty or thirty minutes a day with him." Her grandmother piled the dishes in the sink. "If I don't have time, John takes over. Blue is used to both of us."

John was a retired police officer who lived in Courtenay. He told great jokes and always carried a handful of toffees in his pocket. Dad called him "the significant other." Mom politely referred to him as her grandmother's "friend." Erin wished everyone would just call him a boyfriend. Because that's what he was.

After filling the kettle and putting it on the stove, Grandma sat back down. "Now," she said, resting her elbows on the table and leaning forward. "I have a proposition for Erin." Her eyes gleamed.

Dad groaned. "Not another one!"

Erin giggled. Every summer her grandmother came up with propositions—things she could do to amuse herself while she visited. Once, Erin had stripped old furniture and sold it at the local flea market. Another year, she'd made tapered candlesticks out of the beeswax from Pederson's farm. Both times Erin had gone home with over fifty dollars. Excitement fluttered in her stomach. Earning money was one way to show responsibility. Especially if she managed to save it all and not spend it.

"Steven!" Grandma raised her eyebrows in a mock warning. "Hear me out."

"Do we have any choice?" Erin's father muttered good-naturedly. Mom gave him a playful slap on the knee.

"Something's come up with Duchess," Grandma began. "You remember Duchess?"

They all nodded. Duchess had been born the same year as Blue. Peggy Morris had placed the yellow Lab with a family in Comox. "The Andersons decided to breed her, which was fine with me, providing they honored our contract and allowed me the pick of the litter. But just a week after the pregnancy took, Mrs. Anderson's mother became gravely ill. The family flew back to England to be with her."

Erin frowned. What did all of this have to do with her?

"I agreed to take Duchess," Grandma continued. "I'll look after her through the pregnancy and make sure the puppies get a good start. They're due in three weeks. Sometime around July 27."

Suddenly Erin understood. Her grandmother was going to give her one of Duchess's puppies! She hugged her knees to her chest and began to rock back and forth in anticipation. Finally, a dog of her own to love!

"What does this have to do with Erin?" Dad asked.

Grandma raised her eyebrows again. "I'm getting to that," she told him. "Just hear me out."

"All right." He held up his hand. "I'll wait."

Erin and her mother exchanged grins. Oil and water. That's what her mother called them. Her grandmother was so blunt and her father was so impatient that sometimes when the two of them got together, they just didn't mix.

"I want to show Blue this summer," Grandma explained. "I took him into the ring last year and he did very well. He has the makings of a champion but he needs to accumulate points. I was going to do it, but I'm going to be busy with Duchess and the puppies. I thought Erin could get used to working with Blue and take him into the ring for me. There are several shows this summer—one in Campbell River and a couple here in Courtenay. The one I really want him to enter is being held in Comox on August 12."

Disappointment licked at Erin's insides. Her

smile slipped. She wasn't getting a puppy after all. And it didn't sound like she was going to make any money, either.

Mom sensed her disappointment and gave her an encouraging smile. "What an opportunity, Erin!"

She didn't say anything. She would have taken such good care of it. Her very own dog. Sleeping beside her bed. Going for walks around the neighborhood. Like she'd always wanted.

"It *would* be an opportunity for Erin, but it would also help me out," Grandma continued. "The more ribbons Blue takes, the better. I know Blue is a champion but the rest of the world doesn't. As a breeder, it would be a real feather in my cap to have certified champion stock." She smiled.

The show ring. Who cared about the show ring?

"A few dog shows would keep Erin out of trouble, that's for sure." Dad seemed amused.

Grandma frowned. "You don't understand, Steven. This is serious business. Erin would have to work very hard. She'd have to train with Blue every day. Get used to grooming him, handling him. Have him get used to taking orders from her. It's a great deal of responsibility."

Responsibility? Erin's ears perked up. Maybe she could tolerate the show ring after all.

"By the end of the summer, Erin would know plenty about dogs, and not just about Blue. Not only that, she'd be used to handling herself in front of hundreds of people. It's a tremendous responsibility," Grandma repeated.

It wasn't the job she wanted at the SPCA, but it was something. "You're always telling me I have to be responsible if I want a pet," she reminded her parents.

Her mother nodded. Her father frowned. "Erin's a bit of a daydreamer," he pointed out. "I'm not sure she's—"

"Steve!"

"Dad!" She'd lost out on the SPCA; she didn't want to miss out on this, too.

"Don't underestimate Erin," Grandma said. "She may be dreamy at times, but she's capable and hardworking."

Erin felt excitement spreading through her like water through a hose. "That's right. I *am* hardworking. I like to daydream a little," she glared at her father, "but I work really hard. And if I had my own dog, I'd look after him really, really well." She couldn't resist adding that last bit.

"Mind you, Erin, Blue is far from perfect." Grandma bit the inside of her lip as she studied the animal. "He still surprises me sometimes. You'd have to learn to concentrate on him. Anticipate what he's going to do next."

"Erin can do that," Mom said. "Can't you, sweetheart?"

She nodded. "For sure! And I am tall for my age. It's not like I'd look like a little kid in the ring or anything." For once being too tall might be a good thing. As long as she didn't trip over her feet when she walked Blue in front of the judges.

Her grandmother turned to her. "We'll have to buy you some ring clothes, of course. A nice skirt or a dress. New shoes."

She gulped. She hadn't counted on wearing a skirt. Maybe she could get a long one to cover her legs.

"Tell you what," Grandma continued. "After your parents leave, work with Blue and see how it goes. John and I will show you what to do. If you catch on, and if Blue cooperates, then we'll let you do a few shows."

Erin jumped up from her chair and threw her arms around her grandmother's neck. "You won't be disappointed, I promise you." She gave her a squeeze. "I'll work hard and concentrate. Blue is good. So good, he'll probably take first place."

Her grandmother laughed and returned her hug. "Just do your best, darlin'. Just do your best."

But Erin wasn't listening anymore. She imagined

she was in the show ring, with Blue. Wearing pants, of course!

Sound in the arena would die down. All eyes would turn to her...and glorious Blue beside her. There would be an announcement, of course. "Introducing Erin Morris showing Mr. Lavender Blue. Bred by Peggy Morris of Dove Creek Kennels." She would move slowly but confidently. With Blue prancing elegantly beside her. Turning and stopping when he was supposed to, his head and tail held high and proud. Performing perfectly. Taking first place!

Erin smiled. So what if she had crater claws or ugly legs? Blue would be the perfect one. And she would be right beside him.

Later, her grandmother's phone would ring and ring and ring. People would be begging her to walk their dogs, train their dogs. They'd pay her for it. Her picture would be in the paper and everyone would see it. The SPCA would give her the volunteer position back. Deryk Latham would stop calling her Beast and call her Brains instead. Even Rachel would be impressed.

It would be perfect. And after that, she'd get a dog of her own to love! Her parents wouldn't be able to say no.

Chapter Four

CRIN COULDN'T WAIT to see the dogs her grand-mother had in the kennel run. While her parents cleaned up after lunch, her grandmother went for a quick kennel check and Erin eagerly went along to help.

"You'll see some changes this year." Grandma led her through the fruit orchard and the small veg-etable garden to the building that housed the dogs. "John's been busy." Peggy's voice carried in the wind and the dogs in the kennel began barking when they heard her. "Okay, fellows," her grand-mother called as she crossed the grass. "I'm comin'." She jangled her keys.

Erin smiled. Male or female, they were all "fellows" to her grandmother.

"I've got six dogs here right now." Grandma led the way into the building. "Two young dogs from my last litter and three boarders. Including Duchess."

The kennel had been painted. Instead of its usual gray color, it was pale blue with navy trim. And there were new gates on each of the runs, as her grandmother called them. Even though they were long enough to run in, they were still cages to Erin. And though she knew her grandmother treated her animals very well, it bothered her that the dogs were confined. If this were her kennel, she'd have all the animals in the house!

A full-sized yellow Labrador wagged her tail when her grandmother stopped outside run number one.

"Hello, sweetheart." Grandma unlocked the door and smiled at Duchess. "Come on," she urged Erin inside the cage and then shut the door behind her. "You'll get a run later this afternoon, Duchess." Her grandmother bent down and scratched the dog behind her ears. The Lab's pink tongue licked her grandmother's cheek in appreciation.

Around them, the other dogs howled for attention. The familiar noise made Erin smile. She might not be working at the SPCA this summer, but this was the next best thing. She gestured to Duchess, a short-haired, golden version of Blue. "She's so quiet."

"Always has been." Grandma encouraged Duchess to lie on her blanket. "Dogs have their own personalities, just like we do." Gently she began rubbing and pressing the Lab's stomach.

"Can you feel the puppies?" Erin asked.

Shaking her head, Peggy gave Duchess one last scratch behind the car before she stood up. "Not enough to tell how large the litter will be. Maybe next week. Right now I'm just looking for any unusual lumps or bumps."

"Hi, Duchess." Erin bent down and gave the docile Lab a hug. "How're you doing?" She was rewarded with a large, wet kiss that missed her nose but hit her cheek and ear instead. She laughed and wiped her face.

Her grandmother headed for run number two. "Next is Butch." The black Flat-Coat was bouncing against the gate, his tail wagging fiercely behind him. "He's from the first litter I ever bred," she said proudly. "His owners bring him back every summer when they go south. He needs lots of exercise, this one. Okay, Butch, there's a good boy." Her grandmother pulled something from her pocket, stuck her hand through the cage, and gave the dog a milk bone.

"I can exercise him," Erin offered eagerly.

Grandma shook her head. "His time is right before dinner." She walked toward her double run. "This is Pharaoh and his sister, Star." She unlocked the cage and went inside. "They're just five months old." The two Flat-Coat puppies threw themselves at Peggy, whimpering and shaking and licking her face.

One was liver-colored; the other was black. They looked just like Blue, only smaller.

"They're gorgeous!" Erin bent down and held out her hand. One of the puppies cautiously sniffed her fingers. Then, deciding that Erin was perfectly acceptable, it crawled into her lap and stared up at her with large, soulful eyes. The second dog waited for his milk bone before bounding over to Erin and eagerly snarfling through her hair. A taste of cotton-candy happiness filled Erin's mouth. How she wished she could have a dog of her own to love! She pulled the two dogs close and buried her nose in their fur. They still had that fresh puppy smell.

A mournful howl pierced the kennel and Erin frowned. "What was that?" she asked. It didn't sound at all like a Retriever.

"That's Abby." Her grandmother rolled her eyes good-naturedly. "John's daughter's dog. I agreed to take her while they went back to Saskatchewan for a family reunion. Come on," she urged. "You've never seen anything like Abby before."

Erin gave Pharaoh and Star one last hug and followed her grandmother to run number four. Abby was a two-year-old Beagle that could jump almost as high as Erin's shoulders. She laughed out loud as the dog twisted and twirled in front of them, howling the whole time. "She looks just like Snoopy."

"She's a handful, this one." Grandma stretched her hand through the cage and offered the dog a milk bone. "If she'd been socialized better as a pup, she wouldn't bark so darned much. She's friendly, mind you, and very affectionate." She gave the dog's nose a scratch. "It's time for a run, isn't it, Abby?"

It was the chance Erin had been waiting for. The chance to show her grandmother that she'd be perfect in the ring with Blue. "Can I exercise her, Grandma? Please!"

Grandma hesitated. "I don't know. She can be hard to handle, this one."

"Dogs always behave for me," she said confidently.

Grandma studied her for a minute. "Okay then." She took down the leash that hung on the cage. "Let's give it a try."

But Abby didn't behave at all. The Beagle was impossible! Erin tried to get the animal to do just one thing on command, but the dog would not cooperate. First, Abby ran in mad circles around her feet. Then, she barked at the birds. Finally, when Erin tossed the Frisbee, Abby grabbed it, ran between her legs and barked at her from behind. At first it was funny, but not when Erin realized her parents had come outside and had joined Grandma to see what all the commotion was about. Erin was embarrassed at how little control she had over Abby. Maybe showing dogs wasn't going to be as easy as she thought.

"She's not like Blue, that's for sure." Her grand-mother snapped the leash on a panting Abby when the exercise period was over. "Once you learn a few basic handling techniques, it will come more easily," she reassured her.

"Look at it as good training for the SPCA, bug-face." Dad gave her an encouraging smile.

Erin chewed nervously on the inside of her lip. So much for doing a perfect job with Abby. At least Blue would be easier. She hoped!

"Give me a call when you want to be picked up," Erin's mother said as she pulled up in front of Cassie's house the next morning. "Have fun."

Erin leaned over and gave her mother a quick kiss on the cheek. "Thanks for bringing me over, Mom."

"No problem." She smiled. "Say hi to Cassie's mom for me."

The old beige entrance stairs needed paint just like they had last year—and the year before that. Some things never changed.

Cassie opened the door before she could knock. Erin stared, shocked. Cassie, her summertime friend who had been the same for as long as she could remember, wasn't the same at all!

"It's me, silly!" Cassie grinned and pulled her inside. "What do you like more? My ear cuff or my hair?"

"I'm...I'm not sure!" She tried to grin back but her face was stuck. Cassie wasn't even wearing her usual jeans. This was weird. "They're both so...so... different!" She managed a weak smile.

Cassie spun around and her black minidress flared out from her legs. But this time her long red hair didn't fly out with her. It stayed short and neat against her head. "They cut it even shorter at the back. See?"

Her friend's hair was tapered to a neat V at her neck. "Wow, Cass, you always swore you'd never cut it." Cassie's long hair was as much a part of her as the horses she loved to ride and the Nancy Drew books she loved to read. "What happened?"

"Grade eight happened, silly. Junior high." Cassie rolled her eyes. "It's way different than elementary school."

Cassie was a year older than Erin. It was something Erin rarely thought about. Until now.

"Just wait," Cassie continued. "Kids will be looking at you. In my case, they were looking *down* on me.

They were dying their hair purple and ripping their jeans. I looked like a baby beside them. My mom had a fit when I told her I wanted to do that, but I had to do something. Be different. Treena said I needed to do a reinvention. It's kind of like a makeover." She shrugged again. "So I did."

Treena was Cassie's older sister. She was in grade ten. The Glamour Queen, Erin called her. "A reinvention, huh?"

"Since the other kids were wearing jeans, I decided I'd be different and wear skirts and dresses. Mom loved that idea. But when I dyed my hair, she freaked. Then I complained about how they treated me like a baby and Dad went out and bought me an ear cuff like Treena's, and then he and Mom had the hugest fight." Cassie giggled. "Mom was almost purple, she was so mad. But I got to keep it." She stopped talking suddenly and stared up at Erin. "Hey, when did you get so tall?"

She felt it again. That feeling she got when people stared at her. That feeling like she wanted to drop into a big black hole and never come out. "It just sort of happened." She could have told the old Cassie everything. But she wasn't sure about this new version.

"Come on." Cassie grabbed her arm and dragged her down the hall to her bedroom. "I got a new gold-fish named Mr. Phillips. You've got to see him."

Cassie's room was just as messy as usual. Her bed was piled with books, her dresser was piled with clothes, and her riding gear tumbled out of the closet. Even the fat Mr. Phillips happily swam in a fish bowl that was crammed next to Cassie's radio, magazines, two dirty glasses, and a pile of Lip Smackers. Cassie pushed aside some books and the two girls settled on the bed.

"So," Cassie said, crossing her legs and leaning forward, "how is it being tall anyway?"

Erin smiled. In spite of Cassie's reinvention, her old friend was the same. Always getting right to the things that mattered. "Terrible," she confessed. "The boys all tease me and my feet are too big and I forget how tall I am and I sometimes bump into things. Not only that, look at this." She held out her left hand and showed Cassie her knuckle. "Warts. Mom used some natural sassafras oil but it didn't work and she says I have to wait and let them go away on their own."

"Yuck!" Cassie gave her a sympathetic smile. "I had warts on the bottom of my foot once. For a whole summer. At least you don't have to walk on them," she said.

Erin rolled up the hem of her jeans until the bottoms of her legs were showing. "And look," she said.

She wanted to tell Cassie about ugly legs and crater claw and how awful it felt when everyone laughed, but she couldn't get around the lump in her throat.

"I've seen your legs before, Erin."

"Not since I started shaving them. They look way worse now." She stretched her legs out beside Cassie's short, tanned ones. "No matter how often I shave, I've always got this yucky stubble."

"You don't get stubble with the hair-removal stuff my mom uses. At least that's what they say in the ad."

"I know. It's called a depilatory, and my mom won't let me use it. Because of all the chemicals."

"Your mom is such a nature freak."

Suddenly Erin felt like she had to defend her mother. "It's just…you know…cancer runs in her family. Both her parents died from it, and she's… well…obsessive about keeping things natural and about staying out of the sun. I figured a tan would help. I mean, look how *white* they are."

Cassie stared at Erin's legs. "Yeah, you could probably blind people with them."

"No kidding. But Mom shot down the tan too."

"You could try waxing. It's supposed to help with stubble. Would your mom go for that?"

Erin nodded. "She even bought the wax. And I tried. But I practically passed out."

Cassie rolled her eyes. "You're such a wuss when it comes to pain. We could always sedate you and try."

Erin giggled nervously. Sometimes it was hard to tell when Cassie was kidding. "Yeah, right."

"Seriously." Cassie leaned forward; her eyes gleamed with that look of excitement Erin knew all too well. "I have some tranquilizers for my horse. These huge yellow things. One would probably knock you out for, like, four hours."

"And make me barf."

"But you wouldn't feel a thing. I could wax you all the way up to your bikini line and you wouldn't even flinch."

"Why don't you lay me out in the sun while you're at it?" Erin said, playing along now. "Get me started on the tan I'm not allowed to get. Cut off my warts with a butcher knife. Maybe give me a pedicure and manicure too."

"Good idea! Go to sleep ugly. Wake up beautiful. We could call it Sedate 'N' Spa. It kinda has a nice ring to it, don't you think?"

Erin started to giggle. So did Cassie. Pretty soon the two girls were rolling on the bed, holding their stomachs and howling with laughter.

After a minute, there was a loud bang on Cassie's bedroom door. "Must be Erin Morris in there," a cheerful voice yelled through the door. "Hi, Erin."

"Hi—" Erin gasped through bursts of laughter. "Hi, Treena." She could hear the older girl whistling as she headed down the hall to her bedroom.

"Just get a tan and use the cream," Cassie urged. "You know what they say—it's easier to get forgiveness than permission."

"I know."

"You're too much of a suck." But Cassie's smile took the sting out of her words. "You need to stand up to your parents once in a while."

Cassie was right. She always did the right thing, listened to her parents. But now that she wanted them to let her have a dog, doing the right thing was really important. "I'll have to do something. Grandma's talking about buying me a skirt to wear in the ring."

Cassie leaned past the pile of magazines stacked near her fish and pulled out a small red box. "What ring?" She held out a bag full of broken peppermint pieces.

"The dog ring." Erin picked out the largest piece she could find. "If I work hard and if Blue cooperates, Grandma says I can show him this summer. But she wants me to wear a skirt in the ring."

"Your grandma's cool." Cassie helped herself to a candy. "If you're worried about your legs, she'd probably let you wear pants."

The fresh taste of mint flowed through Erin's mouth. "Maybe." She took a deep breath and let the smell fill her nose. "But the look is important, you know. To impress the judges."

Cassie nodded. She'd been to enough horse shows to know exactly what Erin was talking about. "Your parents are only here for a couple of days, right? And then they go back to Vancouver." Cassie knew the routine. Erin's parents always brought her on a Friday and left Sunday morning.

"They leave tomorrow." She didn't like the gleam in Cassie's eye. It was the same gleam she'd had last year when she decided they should raid the Wellspring Apple Orchard.

"So when they leave, we'll start." Cassie's candy clinked against her teeth. "We'll reinvent you just like Treena reinvented me." She cocked her head to the side and studied Erin's hair. "We'll start at the top and work down. We'll change your hair, we'll dump your warts, we'll fix your legs. We'll change lots and lots of things. It'll be a totally new you."

Erin stared at the totally new Cassie. "I'm not sure I want a totally new me," she admitted. "I just want a better me. A perfect me."

Cassie leaned forward until her nose was almost touching Erin's. "Of course you do. Treena will help." She jumped up, grabbed paper and a pen from the pile on her dresser, and flopped back down on the bed. "First we'll make a list. We don't want to miss anything. When is the dog show anyway?" Cassie's pen was poised over the paper.

"A month or so. I don't know for sure."

"Find out," Cassie ordered. "We need to plan this properly." She began to write. "Hair. Face. Warts." She looked up, studied Erin for a minute, and bent her head again. "Eyebrows. Nails. Treena gives great manicures," she said brightly. "Legs." She glanced up, a sly grin on her face. "When I'm finished, you will love yourself!"

"I don't know." In spite of her hesitation, Erin was catching Cassie's excitement. No warts, smooth, tanned legs. Nothing for the kids to tease her about. It would be perfect. She would be perfect. A perfect Erin Morris to go with Blue in the show ring. "How?" she asked Cassie warily.

"Leave that to me," Cassie said mysteriously. "Me and Treena. We'll give you the perfect reinvention this summer. You can wow the judges at the dog show and go home and wow the boys in grade eight."

She groaned out loud. Not Cassie too! "Since when did you get interested in boys?"

Cassie chuckled and looked up. "You just wait, Erin. Grade eight changes things. Lots and lots of things!"

Chapter Five

THE NEXT MORNING, just a few minutes after her parents had packed up and left, Erin heard the crunch of car tires on the gravel outside.

"*Woof!*" Blue jumped up from his bed by the stove and went expectantly to the door.

She followed him. Maybe her parents had forgotten something. She opened the door to check and Blue raced out between her legs.

Her grandmother peered over her shoulder. "It's John," she said with a smile. Erin followed her down the steps to greet him.

John Travers was crouched beside the back wheel of his red Jeep tousling with Blue. "Long time no see, Missy." He smiled; the skin around his blue eyes crinkled. "How's life over there in the big city?" He reached into his jeans, pulled something out and tossed it into the air. "Catch." A small beige square landed smack in the middle of her palm. She grinned. Same old John.

"Life's fine." At least John hadn't said anything about her getting taller. She unwrapped the toffee and put it in her mouth. Things would be fine. Two months in Courtenay wouldn't be so bad, especially when she had Blue to train with. And Cassie to hang out with. They were going on a picnic just a few hours from now.

John pulled a paper bag from the Jeep. "Brought you a present," he said.

Erin flushed with a mixture of pleasure and embarrassment. "Hey thanks!"

"Actually it's a present for you and Blue," John said as she reached into the bag.

Her fingers closed around something metallic. She pulled it out and studied it. It looked like a big metal U with a coiled spring on one end.

Her grandmother beamed. "I never would have thought of it. What a great idea!"

"I thought so." John smiled back.

Erin turned the giant U sideways. That way it looked more like a triangle. She frowned. What was it?

"Shall we tell her?" her grandmother asked.

John chuckled. "Maybe we should make her guess."

"I give up," Erin told them. "What is it?"

"It's called a springer, m'darlin'. It's for bike riding with Blue."

"Oh." She looked at the metal U again. A springer. She couldn't see how it worked—or why she needed it.

"See this end?" John pointed. "You attach this to your bike and then this," His fingers ran down the U and up the other end, "this end has the spring and attaches to Blue's harness. That way he can run beside your bike without getting caught in a leash. And he'll get the exercise he needs to get in shape for the show."

"Last year when I took Blue out, he just ran beside the bike," Erin said.

Grandma nodded. "I know, but traffic has picked up around here," she explained. "And Blue loves to chase birds and things. It's probably a good idea to keep him on his harness when you're out riding."

"Sure." She bent down beside Blue to let him sniff the metal. "What do you think, Blue? You going to like running with the springer?"

The dog wagged his tail and rolled his tongue across Erin's face. She smiled. "He approves."

John reached out and gave Blue a quick pat on the head. "I thought he would." He turned to Erin. "I understand it's down to work today."

She nodded and sucked on the sweet caramel.

"Do I have time for a coffee first?" He raised his eyebrows.

"Of course!" Grandma turned to Erin. "Why don't you take Blue into the yard and let him run off some steam? We'll be there soon."

The other dogs were howling and yapping in the kennel but she tried to ignore them as she tossed the Frisbee for Blue. It was hard! She wanted to go right over and let them all out. All except Abby! That dog was too much to handle.

"Go, Blue, go!" Delighted, the dog bounced back and forth, catching and retrieving. Even though it wasn't yet noon, the sun was high and hot in the summer sky. She lifted the hair on the back of her neck and wiped away the dampness.

Fetch and toss. Fetch and toss. Back and forth Blue went. She grew hot just watching him run. She wiped her sweaty palms on her jeans and threw the Frisbee yet another time. If she'd worn shorts like Grandma had suggested, she wouldn't be feeling so hot and sticky right now. But she didn't want anybody to see her white legs. Not even John. Besides, if Blue could race around with all that fur on his body, she could wear jeans.

After a while, the heat got to Blue, too. By the time John and Grandma came back, he was lying at Erin's feet, his body panting with exertion.

"Here you go, boy. This'll cool you off." Grandma

placed a bowl of water on the ground and Blue grate-fully lapped it up. "John will walk you through the routine." She handed Erin a dog leash. "I'm going to clean the kennels. I'll check back in a little while."

John reached into his pocket. Erin expected him to pull out another caramel. Instead he pulled out some dried dog treats. "Bait," he explained as he held the small brown square out to Blue. "You'll need to have bait in your pocket during training and in the ring. Sit, Blue," John ordered.

Blue sat.

"Okay." John nodded.

Gently the Retriever took the treat John offered. His dark eyes remained glued on John's face.

"The first thing you'll want to do before you go into the ring is groom your dog." John reached out to stroke Blue's ears. "We'll go over that another day. And we'll spend some time on anatomy then, too. But today I want to see how you and Blue work together, whether you'll be able to handle him in the ring."

A rush of excitement swept through Erin, and it bubbled in her mouth like those tiny exploding candies she loved. If she did okay, she could actually take Blue into the show ring next month!

"We'll do gaiting first. And Blue will do that on lead. Take the leash and put it on Blue," John instructed.

Erin did as she was told. As soon as the leash snapped into place, Blue stood at attention.

"Good!"

The time went quickly. Erin learned the basic gaiting patterns. She walked Blue in a circle, in a triangle, in a straight line—even in something John called an L pattern. She learned that Blue was supposed to walk slightly in front of her, at the end of the leash. She also learned that she had to be firm with Blue.

"Blue!" She reprimanded as he tried to pull away and chase after the birds again. She jerked on the leash.

Blue ignored her. "*Woof! Woof!*" The birds scattered into the sky. Blue shot after them so quickly that Erin was almost pulled off her feet. "Hey!" She laughed.

"Remember," John reminded her, "while you're holding the end of that leash, you're in charge. And keep your voice stern. Blue has to know you mean business. This isn't playtime."

She nodded. Working with Blue was a lot harder than she'd expected. But at least he wasn't as difficult as Abby.

"Hang in there," John encouraged. "You can't expect perfection right away. It's going to take time."

John motioned for the L pattern and with a sigh Erin brought Blue back into position.

The lesson was almost over when Erin noticed her grandmother returning from the kennel with Abby. Expecting Blue to chase after the small dog, she stopped what she was doing and clenched the leash tightly in her hand. The Retriever stopped too and immediately gave her a puzzled look.

"Keep gaiting him. Put him through his paces," John instructed. Abby's yipping and yapping grew louder as Grandma approached. "There will be lots of other dogs at the show," John said, "and Blue has to get used to the distraction. So do you." Erin started walking with Blue again and, aside from a long look as he passed Abby, the Retriever kept going.

Behind her, Erin heard Grandma trying to control the Beagle. "Abby, no!" Grandma spoke sternly to the dog. "Quiet."

By the time Erin completed one last circuit with Blue, Cassie was standing with her grandmother, laughing at Abby's antics. When the Beagle wasn't twisting and jumping for attention, she tried to get her long nose into Grandma's pocket, where the dog treats were kept. Erin smiled and was about to call out, but John stopped her. "Ignore Cassie for now,

Erin. Just like Blue has to ignore other dogs, you have to ignore other people. Blue takes his cues from you. If you're not paying attention, he won't, either."

Erin knew John wasn't angry—he was simply stating a fact. But she flushed with embarrassment, forced herself to ignore Cassie and kept on going. She seemed to be making one mistake after another.

"We'll do more tomorrow." John unsnapped Blue's leash. Tail wagging, the Retriever immediately ran toward Abby. "It's almost lunchtime and I know you and Cassie have plans."

They *did* have plans. Big plans. They were spending the afternoon at Stotan Falls. And that meant music and secrets and their first picnic lunch. With lots and lots of food.

"I don't know which one I like more," Cassie said when Erin joined her. "Abby or Blue. Look at them. They're both so cute!"

She watched the two dogs play a game of chase. When they came together, their mouths opened and they playfully wrestled each other. "I still like Blue." Erin giggled as Abby got hold of Blue's ear and wouldn't let go.

"How did it go, darlin'?" her grandmother asked.

"It wasn't as easy as I thought," Erin admitted.

"Time and practice," John reassured her. "That's

all you need." He turned to Grandma. "Erin's got what it takes," he said. "She's good with Blue and Blue listens to her. With regular work, I think they'll be fine. I'd register her for the shows."

Erin's stomach flipped. John thought she could do it! She and Cassie exchanged grins.

"Are you sure you want to commit to this, Erin?" Grandma's dark brown eyes were serious. "You're going to have to practice every day. Train hard. You won't have as much free time as you usually do. If I register you and Blue, I don't want you backing out," she added.

"I won't back out, Grandma. And I'm used to working hard." Besides, it would all be worth it if she could convince her parents to get a dog! "I really want to do it, no matter how much training I have to do. And Blue likes me, I know he does."

As if in agreement, Blue barked. Not wanting to be outdone, Abby howled. Erin and Cassie giggled. John and Grandma chuckled.

"I should put them back in their runs." Grandma checked her watch. "It's almost time for lunch."

The two girls exchanged looks. Time to go! "I brought the radio," Cassie whispered to Erin. "And leftover pizza, pasta salad, and two kinds of crackers. Do you have some of that shortcake?"

"Yup. And cold chicken, veggies and dip, and a big thermos of grape punch." Erin turned to her grandmother. "Grandma," she asked. "Do you think I could—?"

"If this is about bringing Abby inside the house, don't even think of it." Her grandmother gave her a mock frown. "Just look what happened when I let Blue come inside. If you had your way, the whole kennel would be in my living room." She gave Erin an exasperated sigh, but there was a twinkle in her brown eyes.

"No, Grandma, that's not it," Erin laughed. "We're off for our swim and I want to take Blue with me." The words rushed out but she couldn't stop them. "I can put him on the springer and he'll run along beside me. He'll be fine. I know he will." She didn't want to be away from Blue even for a minute.

Grandma shook her head. "Not today, Erin."

"Blue's tired," John said. "He had a good run before we started working with him. He needs time to rest."

Blue didn't look very tired to her. Erin watched the Retriever and the Beagle wrestle on the grass. He had more energy than she did.

"Another day," Grandma promised.

"Besides, we have plans to make, remember?" Cassie hissed in her ear. "Reinvention plans."

"Right." Erin grabbed the knapsack she'd left in the shade of the apple tree and led the way to the shed. "I'm not sure about that anymore." She went inside for her bike.

"Why not?" Cassie called after her.

She wheeled her bike out. In the distance she saw Blue's tail droop as her grandmother led his playmate off to the kennel. Giggling softly, she turned to Cassie. "I don't know if I'll have time." Her old helmet was dusty; she gave it a wipe. "You heard what Grandma said. I'm going to have to work with Blue every day. John says I have to learn about dog anatomy and how to groom him. I can't blow this, Cass. I have to do well in the ring. Not only that, Duchess is having puppies." She shook her head. "There's so much going on this summer, I don't think I'll have time to worry about warts and hair and legs and stuff."

Cassie got on her bike. "Then let me worry about it." The two girls headed down the driveway. "Me and Treena."

They cycled past the holly and turned right on Dove Creek Road. They had a long ride ahead of them before they even reached the old logging road that would take them to the falls. But there was just enough wind in the air to cool Erin off if she pedaled quickly and steadily.

"I'll see," Erin finally said. But she wasn't sure the reinvention was such a big deal anymore. Especially if she could convince Grandma to let her wear pants in the ring. Maybe even gloves to hide her warts. Then, when she won the dog show and had her own perfect dog, she'd deal with it all. In time for grade eight.

"Come on," she yelled over her shoulder to Cassie. "Race you!"

Chapter Six

STOTAN FALLS WAS ONE of Erin's all-time favorite places. In the winter when the water level rose and the Puntledge River turned cold and deep, it swept away their picnic spots. But when the water receded in summer, it exposed more than a mile of black slate slabs scattered through the water like chocolate discs on a great big birthday cake.

Erin and Cassie carefully picked their way through the shallows of the river, pushing their bikes over and around the rocks. The mossy surfaces were slippery and the bikes were heavy. Small waterfalls trickled over their feet and licked at Erin's rolled-up jeans. Around them groups of kids laughed and splashed. The girls kept their eyes down, careful not to step into one of the tiny swimming holes that sat just below the surface. Some were shallow but many were not.

They were heading for the base of the big waterfall, just past the rock formation they called the dinosaur spine to their special spot on the marshmallow rocks. In her haste to get around the final turn to the fossil wall and "their" spot, Erin almost slipped. Grabbing at her bike, she caught herself just in time. With a triumphant smile directed at Cassie, she pushed her bike past a mother and young child, and rounded the corner.

Treena was there, stretched out on their rock, her pale body slick with suntan lotion. She waved a languid hand in greeting and silently turned back to her book. Erin frowned and turned questioning eyes to Cassie, but her friend gave her a silent shrug. First-of-the-summer picnics were almost always just for the two of them. They had so much catching up to do.

They leaned their bikes against the slate wall, retrieved their packs, and slowly made their way through the water to a nearby rock. Erin laid down the familiar red plaid blanket and glanced around. Three boys chiseled for fossils nearby. A group of kids laughed as they rode over the falls in an inner tube. She'd forgotten how loud the waterfall was.

"I'm going swimming before I eat." Erin eyed the big pool at the base of the falls. There were a few small kids playing around the edge, but the middle was empty. Good. No one to see the hair growing back on her skinny white legs. She started undressing. She couldn't wait to cool off.

Cassie was a step ahead of her. "What do you think?" She flung her shorts and T-shirt into a heap and posed on the blanket with one arm on her hip and the other behind her head. "Like it?"

Cassie's new suit was a bubblegum pink bikini with a gold chain hanging low at the hip. But it wasn't the color or the chain that caught Erin's eye. It was Cassie's body inside the bikini. Cassie had developed breasts. Just like Rachel.

"Nice," Erin mumbled, suddenly self-conscious. She must be the only flat-chested twelve-year-old on the planet! Even the new bathing suit didn't make her happy now. It had looked great at the store but beside Cassie's flashy pink one, it was pretty boring.

Erin turned away, folded her jeans and reluctantly pulled her shirt over her head. She folded it slowly, then placed everything carefully in a neat, little pile. By the time she was done, Cassie was paddling around the swimming hole.

"Come on!" her friend yelled. "Don't be such a slowpoke."

The first rush of cold water took her breath away. Cassie splashed her, and Erin's discomfort faded. So what if Cassie was developing? She was a whole year older. She splashed her friend back and dunked her head below the water. It felt good to cool off after that workout session with Blue and the long bike ride.

More than an hour passed before Treena called out. She was lonely and hungry, she said. By then, Erin was too hungry to care how she looked in her suit.

"This is some kind of spread." Treena grinned and unwrapped wedges of cheese, grapes, and vegetable turnovers—her contribution to their lunch. "There's enough here for six."

Cassie flopped down beside her sister and flicked on the radio. "If Chad shows up, we'll need enough for six," she said, grabbing a chicken leg and biting into it. "Can you hear that?" She gestured to the radio.

"No," Erin and Treena responded in unison. Every year Cassie insisted on bringing the radio in spite of the fact that it couldn't be heard over the falls.

Erin pulled the plaid blanket close to the two girls before helping herself to a slice of ham and pineapple pizza and a carrot stick. "Who's Chad?" she asked.

"Treena's boyfriend." Cassie gave Erin a sly grin. She licked some barbecue sauce from her fingers.

"He's not my boyfriend." A lone fly buzzed close to the pasta salad and Treena shooed it away. She began putting food on a plate. Her long nails, painted fuchsia pink to match her bathing suit, gleamed in the sun.

"He's a boy and he's a friend." Cassie shrugged. "That makes him a boyfriend in my book."

Treena raised her perfectly arched eyebrows. "Then you're reading the wrong books, Cassandra," she said pointedly.

"Right," Cassie muttered. She finished her chicken and dished out some pasta salad.

Erin hid her smile behind the last of her pizza. Cassie hated being called Cassandra and Treena knew it.

"So what's new with you this year, Erin?" Treena popped a cracker into her mouth.

Erin thought right away about Beauty and the Beast but she hesitated, not sure she was comfortable telling Treena-the-Glamour-Queen her problem.

Cassie could read her mind. "It's okay," she said. "Treena's cool."

And so Erin told her about Rachel's crush on the Oresti twins and the problem of Deryk Latham and Beauty and the Beast. She told her about winning the SPCA contest, about her father losing his job and how he'd gone with her mom to the disgustingly healthy camp, which meant she had to spend the whole summer with her grandmother. She told

Treena that Duchess was pregnant and now she was taking Blue into the show ring.

"That's why Erin needs a reinvention," Cassie said.

"Any time." Treena nibbled on a carrot. "Reinventions are my specialty."

"Thanks," Erin said politely. "But I'm not sure I'll—"

"I thought I smelled food." The voice was deep and full of laughter. A tall blond wearing cutoffs and a gray sweatshirt smiled at them. Actually he smiled at Treena.

"Chad!" Treena brightened. "Sit down and help yourself. There's lots."

Erin glanced at the remains of their picnic. They'd been so hungry they'd polished off everything but a lone slice of pizza, a few crackers, traces of pasta salad, and some fruit.

"Here." Treena handed her overflowing plate to Chad. "I saved you some."

Chad sat down beside her. "Thanks." With his dark blue eyes and easy smile, he reminded Erin of her next-door neighbor, Bruce.

"You're welcome!" Treena looked entranced as Chad took a huge bite out of a vegetable turnover.

Erin and Cassie exchanged grins. "See?" her friend mouthed.

She nodded.

"Mark and Robert are fishing upriver." Chad picked up a napkin and wiped his lips. "They'll be down after a while."

Cassie groaned. "That'll give me indigestion for sure." She grabbed the fruit and stood up. "Come on. Let's leave the lovebirds alone."

Treena glared at her sister but said nothing. Chad was so busy eating his pizza Erin was sure he hadn't heard.

"Who are Mark and Robert?" Erin asked when they were finally settled on another rock closer to the falls.

"Chad's fifteen-year-old brother. And one of his friends." Cassie fiddled with the radio dial. "They're real pains. Especially Mark." She was silent as she selected a station. Erin wasn't sure how Cassie could hear anything over the waterfall but eventually her friend seemed satisfied. "Even Treena agrees with me." She turned back to Erin. "The guy's got a problem."

Laughter drifted toward them and Erin glanced back at Chad and Treena. Chad had removed his shirt, and the two of them were stretched out on the blanket together sharing a drink. Erin didn't care whether Chad was Treena's boyfriend or not. She was just glad he had come because now she and

Cassie could be alone, like they usually were for their first picnic of the year.

Erin and Cassie talked for the rest of the afternoon. They traded secrets and dreams. They discussed going into grade eight and what it was like getting older. They chatted about the reinvention and why Cassie liked boys. After a while Erin swallowed her shyness and told Cassie she was lucky she had breasts. Cassie told her not to worry and predicted that she would have breasts bigger than hers by next summer. They even whispered and giggled about Chad and Treena—especially when Treena put sunscreen on Chad's shoulders. They timed her. It took her four minutes and thirty-seven seconds. Probably some kind of record, Cassie suggested. And Erin had laughed so hard she'd gotten the hiccups.

They were just starting to pack up when Erin heard the voices. Cassie heard them too. "Oh no," Cassie said. "It's Mark and Robert. Hurry up," she said. "Let's go."

Cassie wrapped up the last of the fruit while Erin grabbed the plastic containers and stuffed them into her knapsack.

"Leave some for us!" yelled someone who looked like Chad. That must be Mark, Erin decided as the boy came closer. He carried a fishing rod over one shoulder and a tackle box in his free hand.

"Yeah," agreed the second, who was also weighed down with fishing gear. He was shorter, with dark hair and a friendly face.

"Too late," Cassie hollered back. "Your brother ate it all up."

Erin picked up the blanket and gave it a shake.

"At least we're not too late for the fashion show." Mark leaped from rock to rock until he was just behind Cassie. "Whaddya think, Rob?" He eyed Cassie up and down. Cassie couldn't see his eyes but Erin could. He had mean eyes. Deryk Latham eyes. "In the bathing suit competition, I'd give this one an eight. How about you?"

Robert smirked and moved through the water to join Mark. "Kind of skinny," he said, hoisting his rod higher on his shoulder. "I'd say a seven."

Cassie spun around and glared at them. "Get lost," she hissed. "Nobody invited you."

"Okay, okay." Mark held up his hands and grinned. "An eight point five. The bathing suit's nice. Real nice." His eyes skimmed Cassie. "Another year or two and you'll look as good as her." He jerked his head toward the falls where Treena and Chad were splashing each other.

"Come on, Cass." Erin threw a corner of the blanket at her friend. "Help me so we can get out of here."

"Don't be in such a hurry." Mark's eyes turned to Erin. "The competition's not over yet."

The girls began to fold the blanket. Mark jumped over two rocks to get behind Erin. She felt his eyes on her neck, her suit, the back of her legs. Why hadn't they gotten dressed before they started cleaning up?

"This one's not going to make it," Mark said to Robert. "Not in that old-lady bathing suit. Nice hair though. Especially on those white legs of hers." He hooted. There was a burst of nervous laughter from Robert.

Erin clenched her teeth and stared at Cassie. She would not blush. She would *not*. Her friend shot a murderous look in the direction of Erin's shoulder. "Shut up, Mark," Cassie warned.

Mark ignored her. "I'd say a three, Robert. Whaddya think? Hmm?" He didn't wait for Robert's answer. "She might do better in the talent competition, though. Especially if she could do an ape call or two. How 'bout it, Ape Woman? Whaddya think?"

The two boys broke into hysterical laughter.

Erin's face flamed. Her mouth filled with a sharp, bitter taste. The taste of humiliation. She pulled the blanket from Cassie and jammed it into her pack.

Grabbing her jeans and shirt from the rock, she shoved them on top. Forget about getting dressed. She was going home right now! In her bathing suit.

She marched to her bike. She didn't bother looking down or even worrying about her footing. She didn't care if she fell into a swimming hole. Maybe if she was lucky, it would be big enough to swallow her right up.

Cassie came to Erin's rescue just like Rachel did when Deryk Latham got nasty. "At least apes have brains!" she yelled over her shoulder. "Unlike the two of you."

Mark hooted again but Robert was silent.

"Ignore him," Cassie said, joining her. "Like I said before, he has a problem."

A problem. Right. "I'm going, Cass. You can catch up." Erin turned her bike to the river and pushed it through the shallows.

"Hold on, I'm coming." She zipped up her shorts, slung her knapsack over her shoulder, and grabbed her bike.

"Hey, you guys!" Treena yelled from the river.

But Erin and Cassie didn't answer. They didn't even glance back. Instead they slipped and slithered as fast as they dared over the mossy rocks that would take them away from Stotan Falls and back to the safety and silence of Dove Creek Kennels.

Chapter Seven

ERIN WAVED TO CASSIE and slowly wheeled her bike toward the shed. There was a car in her grandmother's driveway—a navy blue sedan parked beyond the holly in the shade of the evergreen tree. Her grandmother had company. Good! She'd be too busy to talk. Erin just wanted to hide.

Quietly she let herself into the kitchen. She could hear her grandmother talking in the living room. If she was lucky, she could tiptoe down the hall to her bedroom where she could pull the blankets over her head and forget all about apes and beauty contests and horrible boys named Mark.

But Erin hadn't counted on Blue.

He heard the door creak. With a welcoming *Woof,* he bounded out from the living room and threw himself at her, his tongue playing over her cheek and down her chin.

"Okay, okay!" Erin dropped to her knees, wrapped her arms around his neck, and buried her face in his black fur. Blue didn't care what she looked like. He loved her no matter what.

"Is that you, m'darlin'?" her grandmother called.

So much for hiding! "It's me." She gave Blue's haunches one last rub before going into the living room. "I'm still wearing my swim stuff," she apologized, self-conscious all over again.

"Doesn't matter." Grandma smiled. "Come and meet Sheila Jones." She gestured to the plump woman sitting on the chair opposite. Cups and a plate of cookies were scattered on the coffee table between them. "She's an old friend and interested in buying one of Duchess's puppies."

"Hello." Erin stood awkwardly in the doorway and nodded at the woman. She was almost formal, in a pale yellow dress and high heels. Quite out of character for most of her grandmother's friends, who favored jeans and sweats.

"How delightful to meet you." Sheila Jones beamed. "I knew your father when he was your age. You look just like him."

Great. Now she looked like a fifty-one-year-old man. She tried to smile. "I really should get dressed." She glanced longingly down the hall.

"Nonsense," Sheila Jones responded heartily. "You look lovely. I must say it's terribly refreshing to see a young person wearing an appropriate swim-suit. So many of them appear almost naked these days. It's quite frightful, really. But you look very respectable." She nodded approvingly. "I could almost see myself wearing something like that."

Suddenly Erin hated her navy blue bathing suit. Her old-lady suit. That's what Mark had called it. And Mark had been right.

Her grandmother caught Erin's eye and gave her a wink. Don't mind her, Grandma seemed to be saying.

She took a step backward, ready to bolt down the hall to the safety of her bedroom.

But Sheila Jones wasn't finished yet. "Yes, you do look like your father when he was a child. Only much prettier, of course." She turned to Erin's grand-mother. "I must say, old girl, you do know how to turn them out. Beautiful children and beautiful dogs." She chuckled at her own joke. "You've got that standard of perfection down to a T."

I'm perfect, all right, Erin thought. Perfectly awful.

Mrs. Jones turned back to Erin. "I understand you're taking Blue into the ring this summer." She clasped her hands together. "When I judged dog shows, the look of the handler was just as important as the look of the dog. You have such a pretty smile and...well, your posture needs work...but if you improve that, and wear the right kind of clothes, I'm sure you'll score highly."

Grandma smiled. "Erin and I are going shopping," she said.

"Good." Mrs. Jones beamed. "I can just see you in a lovely dress, impressing all those judges."

As far as Erin was concerned, the words *lovely* and *dress* didn't belong in the same sentence.

"Of course, keeping control of the dog is important, too, but you look like a big, strong girl," Mrs. Jones gushed. "I'm sure you'll do fine."

Now she was a big, strong girl who looked like a fifty-one-year-old or maybe an ape woman, depending on your point of view. This was so not her day.

"Go ahead and change, darlin'." Grandma must have sensed that Erin yearned to escape. "We won't be long here."

"Not at all," Sheila added. "I was just telling your grandmother that I want another yellow Labrador just like my Radcliffe. The best of the litter, he was. A show dog if there ever was one. And that's what I'm looking for again. Another one that meets the standard of perfection for the breed."

"Of course." Grandma straightened in her chair. "You know I pride myself on the lines I breed. The aim, of course, is the best possible puppies. As close to perfection as possible."

"Wonderful." Mrs Jones nodded vigorously.

"Duchess was paired with a sire from Milwaukee," Grandma continued. "An outstanding dog, really. They make a fabulous match. I'm expecting the entire litter to be show material. I'm sure you'll be completely satisfied."

Erin fled. Down the hall she raced, grabbing the portable phone as she went. She was used to her grandmother's practicality when it came to her breeding program, but all of a sudden it hit her. Standard of perfection. That was her problem. She didn't have one. And they would judge the way she looked in the ring, too!

Her grandmother didn't tolerate imperfections in her pups. Oh sure, she loved them all and she made sure they all had very good homes, but Erin knew her heart was with those puppies that had the standard of perfection down to a T.

Blue would be perfect at the dog show. Just perfect. And she would be right beside him, maybe ruining his chance to come in first.

She couldn't let that happen.

Quickly Erin dialed the familiar number. Her parents thought she was perfect the way she was. Well, they were wrong. She wasn't perfect…not yet. But after the reinvention, she might be.

Too bad if she was going to be busy training Blue. She had to make time for the reinvention. For the sake of the dog show. For Blue. And to stop people like Deryk and Mark and girls with Vuarnet sunglasses from talking about her. Stop them once and for all.

She listened to the phone ringing on the other end of the line. Impatiently she tapped her fingers on the bedspread. "Hurry up and answer, Cassie," she spoke out loud. "The on-again, off-again reinvention is definitely on!"

Erin stared at the list in front of her.

"Well?" Cassie leaned across her kitchen table and tapped the paper with a slim blue pen. "What do you think?"

"It looks pretty good." Erin sipped her root beer and read the list again. *Pluck eyebrows. Fix hair and legs. Get rid of warts on knuckle. Buy new clothes. New bathing suit. Learn to walk without tripping.* It was a lot to do, but they had almost a month until the dog show. "I don't know about the self-tanner or the depilatory." Cassie had both things on the list. "You know how my mom is about chemicals."

Cassie's eyes flashed with annoyance. "That was before Mark said all those awful things to you. Come on, Erin. Your Mom may be a health nut but she's not totally unreasonable."

"Yeah, I know." Their picnic was four days ago but Erin could hear Mark's words like he was yelling them from Cassie's living room. *Ape Woman.* An *old-lady bathing suit.* A *three.*

"You won't go for the Sedate 'N' Spa, so waxing is out. You could try skipping the sunscreen, but I don't how much of a natural tan you'd get in two weeks. The self-tanner is the only answer."

Erin picked up the bottle and read the list of ingredients. One chemical after another. "Mom's probably never seen a bottle of this stuff before. I guess I could ask and play dumb about what's in it." Her mother wasn't stupid—she'd probably know—but it was worth a shot.

"Okay. How about we leave the legs for now and start with your hair? Or your warts?"

Erin brightened. "My warts," she said firmly. "Let's do those first."

Cassie grabbed Erin's hand and studied her knuckles. "Maybe we could just cut them off?" she suggested.

She pulled her hand back. "No way. You know

how I am with pain." She gave Cassie a sheepish grin. "Besides, I tried it a few months ago. It didn't work."

"I read a book about spells once, and it said you could rub all sorts of things on warts to make them go away," Cassie said.

"Like what?"

"Toenails. Garlic. Even Pepsi."

Erin wrinkled her nose. "Gross. I thought you said your mom has some wart stuff?" Cassie's mom wasn't the natural medicine nut Erin's mother was.

"Right!" Cassie stood up and pushed her chair back. "Come on."

Cassie's bathroom was cheerful and cluttered. It had blue and white towels, a shower curtain covered with brightly colored fish, and a vanity that held bottles of hand cream and perfume. It wasn't particularly large, but it gave Cassie and Erin just enough room to move.

"Here it is." Cassie pulled a tiny bottle filled with clear liquid from the cupboard. "Wart Away." She read the fine print on the back. "It says to use it every day for a week and then stop." She looked at Erin. "You'll have to take it home," she said. "Or else come over every day."

Erin grinned and nodded. Finally her warts would be gone!

"Are you ready?" Cassie unscrewed the cap.

She nodded a second time. No more crater claw for her. She held out her hand and watched as Cassie filled the dropper full of the clear liquid and positioned it over the biggest wart.

Drip. Drip.

"Oww!" She flinched.

"Sit still!" Cassie ordered. "I haven't gotten the second one yet."

"But it stings!" Erin jerked her hand away and eyed the tiny bottle of Wart Away on Cassie's bathroom counter. "What if it eats through my entire hand?" She stared nervously at the warts on her knuckle.

"It's perfectly safe," Cassie reassured her. "Come on. Let me get them a second time. Just to be sure."

"OWWWWW!" Erin waved her hand madly in the air. "It stings, Cass. Real bad." She clenched her teeth.

Cassie stared at her. "Your face is turning red. I've never seen you—"

"It HURTS!" Erin screamed. "Turn on the water."

Cassie did.

Erin stuck her hand under the tap. Immediate relief. "I'm not using that again," she said when the stinging finally subsided. "No wonder my mom hates chemicals. We'll have to find something else."

Cassie replaced the lid on the bottle of Wart

Away and tucked it back into the cupboard. "How about the garlic?" she suggested.

Erin slid off the bathroom counter and stood on the floor. "The garlic sounds pretty stupid," she said. "I can't believe it'll work."

"It's worth a try," Cassie said. "Come on."

Into the kitchen they went. The early afternoon sun streamed through the windows and turned the pine cabinets a pretty golden yellow. Copper pots hung on the wall beside the fridge. A small clay crock to the left of the stove held one orange shallot and several fat heads of garlic. Cassie picked up one fat head and rolled it on the counter under her palm.

"What are you doing?" Erin glanced nervously toward the living room where she could hear Cassie's mother talking to Treena. Thank goodness they hadn't heard her screaming in the bathroom.

"I'm loosening them." Cassie peeled away the silvery paper and pulled two cloves from the bulb. She grabbed a knife from the drawer and began to cut. "The book says to rub the warts with the cloves, and then plant the cloves somewhere in the garden. When the clove dies, the wart will shrivel up, too."

It was silly but Erin was willing to try anything. Anything that didn't hurt, that is. "What if the clove grows?" she wondered out loud. "Does that mean my wart grows bigger?"

"Cloves don't grow," Cassie said matter-of-factly. "Would anything that smells this bad want to grow bigger?" She held the cut clove under Erin's nose.

Erin sniffed. "I guess not," she said. "What kind of book was this in again?"

"A book on magic spells." Cassie reached for Erin's hand. "I got it out of the library when I was trying to get Jonathan to like me." She held out the cut clove. "Stand still while I rub." She hesitated. "I think I'm supposed to say a spell or something. I can't remember."

There was movement in the living room. It sounded like Treena and Cassie's mother were coming into the kitchen. "Hurry up!" Erin whispered. "Just make something up."

"Okay!" Cassie squeezed her eyes shut. "Wart no, wart flow. With this clove I make you go." Quickly she rubbed the garlic back and forth over Erin's warts. "Go, wart, go."

"What are you girls doing in here?" Cassie's mother smiled at them from the doorway.

"Nothing," Erin and Cassie said in unison. Cassie folded her fist around the clove of garlic and tucked it behind her back.

"Smells like Caesar salad in here." Treena

opened the fridge and peered inside. "But it's too early for salad, I'm still looking for breakfast."

Erin giggled nervously but Cassie frowned. "We're going outside now." She pulled Erin toward the back door. "Bye."

"You've got a mess to clean up," her mother called after her.

"Later," Cassie yelled back.

They wandered away from the house, beyond the flower fields, to a shady corner near some dark red poppies. "We'll plant the clove here," Cassie told Erin, "and when it turns to mush, your wart will, too!"

Erin crouched and started to dig a little hole. "I wonder how long it'll take."

"Longer than a week," Cassie predicted as she helped dig. "I think that's big enough." She tossed in the clove of garlic and began to cover it with soil. "I have to say another spell," she told Erin.

A seagull screeched overhead. Erin jumped. In spite of the warm afternoon sun, she felt cold. The garlic idea had seemed goofy at first, but now it seemed almost spooky. She rubbed nervously at the warts on her knuckle. "Okay," she agreed.

Cassie stared silently at the ground. Finally she looked up. "Got it," she said confidently. Ceremoniously she held a handful of soil above the small hole. "Rot, clove, rot. Go, wart, go. And as you rot, the wart will go." Slowly she let the stream of soil fall. "There!" Cassie patted the ground triumphantly. "You just wait, Erin. Those warts will disappear and you'll never know you had them!"

"I hope so!" Erin watched the seagull glide on the wind before it turned in a slow arc and headed south. She and Cassie followed it.

Cassie gave her a sly grin. "And you wait," she said. "The perfect reinvention is just beginning."

Erin grinned back. Her uneasy feeling was gone. Cassie was right. By the time the dog show rolled around, she'd be the perfect Erin Morris. To go with the perfect Mr. Lavender Blue.

"Today your warts, tomorrow the rest of you."

Erin held out her left hand and stared at her knuckles. Was it her imagination or were the warts already looking smaller? "The rest of me is going to have to wait awhile," she told Cassie. "I've got to train some more with Blue. And then there's clothes shopping to do. For the show." She stopped by her bike. "Maybe you could come," she said, "and help me pick some stuff out."

"Great!" Cassie loved shopping. "When?"

"I'm going to be busy training this weekend,"

Erin said, "so sometime next week. Maybe Tuesday or Wednesday. I'll call you."

"We'll get you a new bathing suit," Cassie said excitedly. "And some cute little tops and—"

"I'm not putting on another bathing suit this summer!" She reached for her helmet and pulled it on.

"Once you change your hair and fix your legs, you'll feel different," Cassie predicted.

Erin snapped the helmet strap in place. "I don't know." Her legs weren't such a big deal. She could spend the rest of the summer in jeans and probably convince Grandma to let her wear pants in the ring too. Then she remembered Mark's taunts at the river a few days ago. Erin was tired of being razzed about how she looked. And her legs were part of it. She stifled a sigh. Maybe Cassie was right. Maybe she should just suck it up and go behind her mother's back. Even though the idea made her feel kind of creepy inside.

Cassie grinned and that mischievous look sparkled in her eyes. "We'll figure something out," she yelled as Erin swung her leg over her bike and pushed off toward her grandmother's house. "See you soon."

Chapter Eight

"LOOK WHAT CAME IN THE MAIL." John waved an envelope at Erin when she walked through the door of the kennel the following Wednesday. "A registration form for the Campbell River dog show. It's running a week after the one in Courtenay. Interested?"

Erin handed John the warm muffins her grandmother had sent out from the kitchen. "Don't think so." She took a blueberry muffin and perched on a stool to eat it. She was still trying to wake up. Her grandmother had said she had a lot to learn today, so she'd gotten her up early.

"Why not?" John asked.

Erin shrugged. She wasn't sure the perfect reinvention would be perfect enough, but she couldn't tell John that. "One show's probably enough for me." She bit into a blueberry and the warm juice filled her mouth.

John put the envelope down. He turned back to the stainless steel bowl where he was mixing up breakfast meal. The dogs were hungry. Abby was howling. Butch was pacing. Pharaoh and Star were throwing themselves against the cage with solid thuds.

"The more shows you do, the more points you accumulate. And the more exposure Blue gets, the better it is for your grandmother."

Erin reached out and scratched Blue behind his ear. The dog's brown eyes were fixed firmly on the muffin in her other hand. "I know," she said. But it would only take one show to prove to her parents that she was responsible enough for a dog. Especially if Blue won. Correction, *when* he won. Besides, that daydream about getting her name in the paper and having people calling to walk their dogs was just a daydream. It didn't really matter. All that mattered was getting her own dog.

"If you get enough points, you could find yourself at the nationals in Ottawa later this year."

"I'd have to get to the provincials first. And do a lot of dog shows." Do them well, too, Erin added silently.

John nodded and began filling individual bowls. "True enough. But I have a friend in West Vancouver who can't show his dog anymore. Has a bad hip. He's looking for someone to take his shepherd on the circuit." He took Abby her food first. When he returned, he said, "Why don't you enter Blue in the Campbell River show? You can always decide later if you want to go in."

Erin handed Blue the last piece of her muffin. The dog practically inhaled it before licking her fingers in search of more crumbs. She giggled as his tongue methodically traveled between her fingers and across her palm. Blue was the best. He deserved to be a champion. A champion twice. And maybe that daydream about getting her name in the paper wasn't a bad one, after all.

"Okay," Erin said. "I'll do it."

"Good!" John gave her a pleased grin. He handed her a few sheets of paper. "Read these over while I hand out breakfast. Then we'll get to work."

"You mean I have to know all of this?" she asked John when he finished the feedings. There was so much material; Erin was worried she wouldn't remember it all. There were sheets on the history of her breed, the rules of the show ring, and photographs of proper form.

"The judges are going to question you about your breed. You never know what they're going to ask, so all you can do is be prepared. Don't worry," John reassured her, "lots of this stuff you already know."

"Lots of it I don't." She re-read the section on

characteristics. "I didn't know Flat-Coated Retrievers were originally from the U.K." She flipped to health. "And I've heard Grandma talk about hip dysplasia, but I didn't know about ear infections. Or skin allergies."

John grabbed a stool of his own and sat beside Erin. "By the time I'm finished with you, you'll know it all."

She looked glum.

"It's all part of the show prep." John's voice was soft but firm. "You're Blue's handler. You're being judged even more than the dog. It's a feather in your grandmother's cap if Blue does well, but he doesn't have to be a top dog. You, on the other hand, need to understand your breed and learn to handle your dog perfectly."

And look good, Erin added silently.

John reached for the papers in her hand. "We'll start with Flat-Coat Retriever history," he said.

Erin was surprised to learn that she did know a lot about Flat-Coats. What she didn't know, John explained. He was a good teacher and he made learning fun. It helped that Blue was with them. If something needed explaining, they had the perfect model right at hand. Time went fast. Erin was shocked when John glanced at his watch and told her more than an hour had gone by. After a long stretch and another muffin, they started in on grooming techniques.

"Show Blue the brush," John instructed. She held the black-handled brush below Blue's nose. He sniffed curiously at the yellow bristles. "That way he knows it's time to be groomed," John explained. He gave Blue a scratch behind his ears before he turned to leave. "Just remember what I said. Start at the top of the head and work back. Pay attention to the feathers, especially on his legs, chest, and tail. Call me when you're done."

Blue's eyes followed John as he walked to Abby's cage and let the small dog out.

"Okay, Blue." Gently Erin began to brush the top of Blue's head. The dog tossed her hand off with the flick of his long, black nose. His tongue came out and licked her knuckles. Her warty, crater claw knuckles. "Stop it!" She tried to frown but she giggled instead. Again his tongue licked her warts. "Blue!" It had been five days since she and Cassie had buried the clove of garlic. The warts looked just the same to her. But no matter how many times she washed her left hand, Blue had developed a real taste for it.

"Be firm," John yelled out. "You're in charge, remember." He was brushing Abby.

"That's it, Blue." She gave the dog a pretend fierce frown. "Sit still and let me groom you." She brushed him with firm, steady strokes. Blue sensed that she meant business. Finally he was still. The only movement was the blinking of his dark eyes as he watched her.

He was so gorgeous with his almond-shaped brown eyes and his jet black fur, she thought as her hands worked the brush. It was impossible to stay mad at him. Even pretend mad. She lifted his head and began on his neck. Blue closed his eyes in pleasure.

Erin tasted caramel apple happiness. For a minute she pretended Blue was her dog, that he would be going home with her after her time in Courtenay. She could see exactly how it would be.

Her father would pull the car onto the deck of the ferry. Her parents would gather their magazines as they prepared to get out. "I'm going to stay below deck," Erin would say. "With Blue." Her parents would give her an approving nod and Erin would settle down with a book. But she would have no time to read, because the men who worked the ferry would stop by the car every few minutes to comment on the ribbons

*her dog wore around his neck. She would intro-
duce him. "Mr. Lavender Blue," she would say.
"A champion. First prize in two dog shows." And
when she was home and Rachel and the Oresti
twins came over and saw Blue lying on the rug
in her living room, she would—*

Something cold touched Erin's wrist. She jumped;
the brush almost flew from her hand. It was Abby,
wagging her tail and checking things out.

"How are you doing?" John asked a minute later.
He crouched down and watched her move from
Blue's stomach to his haunches. "Looking good," he
said approvingly. "When you finish up, I'll show you
how to clean his teeth."

"I don't have to do that at the show, do I?"

John laughed. "No," he reassured her. "But the
judge sometimes wants to look in the dog's mouth.
Blue hates having anyone messing around in there.
He needs to get used to it."

She nodded and went to work on Blue's tail.

Abby put her head between her paws and stuck
her bum in the air. "*Woof!*" The Beagle thought it
was playtime. She tried to get Blue's attention. "You
sit," John ordered. Surprisingly, the Beagle did
exactly as she was told. "I hear your grandmother

has a shopping trip planned for this afternoon." John's eyes twinkled.

She wrinkled her nose. "At least Cassie's coming." On the phone last night Cassie had made the shopping trip sound almost fun.

"Looks like they're pretty anxious to get going." John pointed. Cassie and Grandma were coming through the door. "We'll have to leave the teeth for another day," he said.

"Hi!" Erin grinned and put down the brush. Blue shook with pleasure at being free. Abby ran circles around the two women.

"Hello, darlin'." Grandma moved swiftly through the kennel, reaching out to give the Beagle an absentminded pat. "How's Duchess?"

"She's been really quiet this morning," John responded. "Wouldn't even eat her breakfast."

"Did you bring your money?" Erin whispered as Cassie joined her.

Cassie nodded and the two girls walked toward Duchess's cage. "Mom gave me my allowance early," she whispered back. "You should see my list. It's huge."

"The pups may come early," John said to Grandma when the two girls caught up. Blue was ahead of them, sticking his nose into the cage and whining softly at Duchess.

"When is she due?" Cassie asked.

"Not for another nine days." Grandma unlocked the cage door. Blue rushed in ahead of her, nudged Duchess with the tip of his nose before lying down close beside her. "Look out, Blue." Grandma gave him a gentle push. "Give me some room." Blue stood up, turned in a half circle, and settled down with a *thrump* only a few inches away from Duchess.

Grandma sighed in exasperation but her lips twitched. Stretching past Blue, she palpated Duchess's stomach. The yellow Lab raised her head. But then, as if the effort to keep it in the air was simply too much, she put it back down again. "I can feel five," Grandma said after a minute. "Maybe even six." She rocked back on her heels and glanced at the food and water dishes before turning her eyes back to Duchess. "Everything seems fine but I'd feel better if you'd eat something, Duchess, old girl." She gave Duchess one last rub on her belly before standing up. "Keep an eye on her, John. And keep her water dish full, would you?"

He nodded and hustled Abby back to her pen.

Grandma checked her watch. "We shouldn't be more than a few hours."

"I'm sure we'll find something in this store,"

Grandma assured the girls as she pushed open the door to Alesa's Closet and walked inside.

Erin and Cassie followed. Seconds later, Cassie shifted her parcels from one hip to the other as she started inspecting a rack of skirts. Her grandmother began talking to a tall woman with towering black hair and matching black eyebrows that formed perfect half-moons over her eyes. Erin spotted a chair near the back of the store. Finally a chance to sit down!

The chair was small and hard but it felt wonderful to her. She was tired. She was thirsty. And her feet hurt. She loosened the lace on her running shoe and rubbed her heel. She should have worn socks. She was getting a blister.

"I knew we'd find something here." Her grandmother's face was flushed with success as she joined Erin. "Alesandra has a number of outfits she thinks would work in the ring. She's going to bring them out."

"Would you mind standing, darling? I must get your size." Alesandra had an accent that reminded Erin of her Hungarian neighbor, Mrs. Czas. Reluctantly she stood and tried to be patient while the woman took her measurements. Her huge black hair bobbed and dipped with each movement. Finally she was through. "I will only be a moment." She disappeared through a beaded curtain.

"Will you look at this!" Cassie shoved a bright red shirt under Erin's nose. "It's on sale for fifteen dollars and it's my size." She fumbled in one of her bags before pulling out the shorts she'd bought three stores ago. "Don't you think it would go great with these?"

Erin nodded and feigned enthusiasm. She slipped her runner off and massaged her heel.

Grandma reached for Cassie's find and rubbed it between her fingers. "That's a good-quality cotton." She held it against the new shorts and eyed it critically. "It's not my taste, of course, putting red and yellow together, but I must admit it does pack a punch. At that price you can hardly lose. Why don't you try it on?" she encouraged Cassie with a smile.

"I will!"

I must be the only girl on all of Vancouver Island who hates shopping, Erin thought glumly as she watched her grandmother take Cassie's parcels and shoo her into the dressing room.

"Now then." Alesandra was back. She hung half a dozen items on a rack and began arranging them according to color. Erin studied the woman's hair and tried to decide if it was a wig or if it was real.

"That navy blue set looks lovely, doesn't it, Erin?" Her grandmother didn't wait for an answer. Instead she played with the fabric and asked Alesandra about cleaning instructions.

Navy blue. Erin would die before wearing navy blue again! She shoved her foot back into her runner and winced as the blistered skin rubbed against the canvas.

"What do you think?" Cassie twirled in front of her. She'd put on her new yellow shorts and the red top. Erin had to agree with her grandmother. Together the red and yellow was Day-Glo bright. But on Cassie it looked just right.

"It looks great," she said sulkily. "It really does." Maybe she was just a boring navy blue kind of person.

Cassie studied her for a minute and then knelt down beside her. "What's wrong? You're kinda quiet."

Erin shrugged. "Tired, I guess."

"You need to buy something. That'll make you feel better. Trust me." Cassie turned and eyed the rack of clothes. "Your grandma's right. They have great stuff here. I'm sure you'll find something."

Erin did. But it wasn't the same thing her grandmother liked. "Please, Grandma. Can't we get this?" Erin turned to the right and watched in the mirror as the soft flare of the white pants moved with her. She smoothed the vest top and pulled her shoulders back. "I think it would look great in the ring."

Cassie gave her the thumbs-up sign but her grandmother sighed and turned troubled eyes to Alesandra. "I really wanted something more feminine." She pointed to the navy skirt set. "Something like that."

Gross. "I won't wear navy," Erin said flatly.

Cassie was waving her arms madly in the air. *Don't be so disagreeable*, she seemed to be saying.

But Erin was tired of being agreeable. Tired of being dragged from one store to another. Tired of trying to find just the perfect outfit to wear in the ring. Especially now that she was working on the perfect reinvention. But she couldn't very well tell her grandmother that. Not yet. And not now. Not with Alesandra of the big hair watching her.

"I don't understand what it is with you and navy," her grandmother said mildly.

Erin had a brainstorm. "It's Blue," she said quickly. "He's so dark, he'd look terrible walking beside me if I was wearing navy. He'd look better if I was wearing white." She turned to the left this time and watched the pants flare out from her legs. No one would call her an old lady wearing this.

"She has a point," Alesandra said softly.

Grandma nodded. "Okay," she said slowly. "Pull out everything else that's light in color."

"I like this, Grandma, I really do."

But her grandmother wasn't listening. She was on the phone to John, asking about Duchess and telling him they were going to be later than she'd originally thought.

Finally, after going through Alesandra's entire stock of just about everything that would fit Erin, they narrowed the choice down to three outfits: a pink skirt and sweater, a pale blue dress, and the white vest and pant suit Erin loved so much.

Erin eyed the pink skirt nervously. It was above her knees. "Don't you have any long skirts?"

Alesandra shook her head. "Long skirts don't come in until fall. And then they are usually dark. Not light."

She couldn't wear a skirt in the ring with Blue. Erin just couldn't. Unless it was long. Or unless she did something with her legs.

"We'll be fine with one of these." Grandma held the blue dress against Erin and narrowed her eyes. "A little too formal, I think."

Cassie tilted her head to the side and studied Erin. "Too Alice-in-Wonderlandish."

"Oh, heavens, we can't have that." Grandma was clearly horrified.

Erin hid her smirk. When her grandmother turned to put the outfit back, it was her turn to give Cassie the thumbs-up sign.

"I do like this, though." Grandma held out the pink skirt. "What about you, darlin'?"

In spite of the skirt, Erin liked the outfit, too. It was made of soft cotton, and the sweater had pretty three-quarter-length sleeves.

"It's nice," Erin said cautiously. "But the skirt's kind of short."

Grandma gave her an exasperated look. "For heaven's sake, it's almost to your knees."

To her *white* knees! "What if I have to bend over in the ring or something...?" Erin's voice trailed away. She could tell by the look in her grandmother's eyes she had lost.

"We'll take this." Grandma handed the outfit to Alesandra. She hesitated and then reached for the white pants and vest. "You may as well wrap up this up, too." She gave Erin an indulgent smile. "I'm sure you'll find a use for it sooner or later, even if you don't wear it in the ring."

Erin grinned. Grandma was such a softie. "Thanks, Grandma." She gave her a hug.

"You're welcome, darlin'."

"Way to go," Cassie whispered to Erin as Grandma

paid for the purchases. "Maybe if you work on her some more, she'll change her mind and let you wear the pants in the ring after all."

"Cassie Walker, don't you go puttin' ideas in my granddaughter's head." Grandma's voice rang out loud and clear in the small shop. "I've made my decision and I'm standing by it. It's going to be a skirt in the ring and that's it."

"Whoops!"

Erin grinned and pulled Cassie to the front of the store. She glanced back to her grandmother. She was intent on her conversation with Alesandra. "I'll get John to talk to her. Convince her that the pants are better." Erin kept her voice low. "My dad says John can get her to do anything."

"What are you two giggling about?" Grandma handed Erin a large bag before opening the door and motioning them out to the sidewalk.

"Oh, nothing," Erin said with as much innocence as she could muster. Cassie's giggles grew more intense.

The two girls were still laughing when they reached the car.

Chapter Nine

"JOHN THINKS I SHOULD WEAR the skirt, too." Erin shoved the last of her pepperoni pizza into her mouth and licked her fingers. Cassie's mom finished wiping the counter, reminded the girls to load their plates into the dishwasher when they were done, and wandered away. Erin picked up her mug of root beer. "I heard him tell my grandmother that proper clothing was as important as proper form." She gulped at her drink.

Cassie rolled her eyes. "It's a dog show, for heaven's sake. It's not an audience with the Queen."

Erin snorted. Some of the root beer dribbled down her chin; the rest detoured into her nose. She gasped and laughed and swallowed, all at the same time.

"That was a nose full." Cassie laughed and handed her a tissue for her chin. But then her smile disappeared and her voice dropped. "Adults can be so weird." She jerked her head in the direction of the living room. "Like my mom and this whole makeup thing." Cassie was allowed to wear makeup, but not as much as she wanted to. "She's acting like the makeup police," she grumbled.

Giggling, they got up to rinse their plates. "So what are you going to do?" Cassie asked.

Erin shrugged. "I don't have a choice about the skirt. I have to wear it. So maybe I'll buy white tights or something."

"And roast to death," Cassie teased.

Erin didn't answer. She stared out the kitchen window, secretly relieved to see drizzle falling. It was the first rainy day of the summer. "Look, Cass, it's raining. I guess we can't go to swimming at the falls like you wanted to." She didn't want to go back there anyway. Because she was never putting on a bathing suit in public again.

Cassie peered out the window. "Perfect! Then we'll do your legs today." She opened the dishwasher and stacked their plates on the lower rack. "Mom bought a new bottle of depilatory. I saw it when she unpacked the groceries last night. And I've got a practically full bottle of self-tanner, remember?"

Erin shook her head. "Not today," she said.

"Why not?"

"I haven't talked to Mom yet."

"I thought you were going to call her?"

"I did. Twice. Both times Dad answered. Mom's doing some extra tutoring. And when she called back, I was out walking Blue. We keep missing each other."

"We have to deal with this, Erin." Cassie slammed the dishwasher. "I'm leaving for a week of camping in a few days. That doesn't give us much time for the perfect reinvention."

Erin finished her root beer and rinsed the glass. "Maybe Grandma would understand."

"And maybe she won't," Cassie pointed out. "It's your body. You're the one who's getting teased all the time. Take some control."

"Like you're going to take control and wear all the makeup you want to wear when your mom says no?" Erin responded hotly.

Cassie looked embarrassed. "Okay," she said reluctantly. "I see your point. Besides, if we do your legs now, they'll be hairy and pale by the time the show rolls around. We'll deal with them after I get back from Long Beach."

Anything could happen by then! "Sure," Erin said.

"But I want you to promise me something."

"What?"

"That you'll forget the sunscreen on your legs for the next while."

"How can I forget? Mom gave me gallons of the stuff."

"Man!" Cassie groaned. "You *forget* because you make a *point* of forgetting."

"And what happens when Mom sees me with tanned legs at the end of the summer?"

"What's she gonna do? Take the tan back?"

"After she kills me, she might."

They both laughed.

Treena wandered into the kitchen. Rubbing sleep from her eyes, she peered blearily at Erin and Cassie. "What are you two plotting now?" she asked. Her hair was tousled, her shorts and T-shirt rumpled.

"How was your date last night with your *un-boyfriend* Chad?" Cassie asked, poking Erin with her elbow. Erin swallowed her giggle.

"It wasn't a date," Treena informed her loftily. She smoothed her blonde hair. "And there's no such word as 'un-boyfriend.'" She directed a grumpy frown in the direction of the coffee pot. "What do you have to do to get a morning cup of coffee around here?"

Cassie looked at her watch and then at Erin. This time Erin couldn't help it. Her giggle slipped out. It wasn't morning anymore. She waited for Cassie to make some sarcastic remark. But Cassie surprised her.

"Sit down, Treena," Cassie said helpfully. "I'll make your coffee."

Treena slid into a chair in the nook and yawned. "Okay."

"Is it two scoops or four?" Cassie asked as she filled the kettle with hot water and put it on the stove.

"Four." Treena glanced casually at the newspaper in front of her.

Erin stared at Cassie. Cassie's eyebrows were dancing up and down, and her mouth was moving in some sort of silent message. Erin didn't get it.

Cassie finished scooping the coffee into the cone and slid into the chair beside her sister. "Want something to eat, Treen?" Erin took the chair closest to the window.

"Sure, I'll have a muffin if there's one around." Slowly, Treena's head rose from the newspaper. Her blue eyes narrowed suspiciously. "What do you want, Cass?"

Cassie had a who-me? look on her face. She made a fuss unwrapping a carrot muffin and sliding it in front of her sister. "Okay," she admitted, "I want you to cut Erin's hair."

"What?" Erin yelped.

"Erin needs her hair cut," Cassie continued.

"No, I don't!"

Cassie ignored her. "Just an inch off the bottom. You used to do mine all the time. Please, Treena?"

Treena glanced over to Erin. "Do you want your hair cut?"

Erin glared at Cassie. It was just like her to spring this on her with no warning at all. "No," she said defiantly. "We were going to *fix* my hair. Not cut it!"

Cassie was undeterred. "Cutting *is* fixing." Her face had that I've-made-up-my-mind look. "It's for the reinvention we were telling you about," she reminded Treena, "to make Erin perfect for the dog show. And I thought if you shaped her hair—*just a little*—then the henna would work better and—"

"Henna!" Treena and Erin spoke in unison.

Vigorously Cassie nodded her head. "I thought we'd try henna on your hair. I bought it yesterday at the superstore. You can pay me back whenever you want," she added generously. "No rush." She looked particularly pleased with herself.

The kettle began to boil. Treena stood up and poured the water through the drip.

Erin leaned back until her chair was touching the wall. How typical of Cassie to make plans without even asking her. "We didn't talk about henna or cutting my hair or anything like that," she said crossly.

"We did—you just don't remember. Anyway, it was all my idea," Cassie bragged. "And you're going to love it, trust me."

Trust me. Those words had gotten her and Cassie into trouble ever since Erin had been coming to Courtenay for the summer. Like the time they had given Cassie's cat, Zeus, a buzz cut. The cat had squirmed, the razor had slipped out of Erin's hand, and the poor animal had ended up looking like something out of a horror movie. It had taken a full year for the fur to grow back. Even now Zeus ran every time Erin even looked at him.

"What's henna, anyway?" Erin asked.

"Remember? It's that Egyptian plant dye stuff," Cassie said excitedly. "In some parts of the world, they put it on their hands and the bottoms of their feet, too." Her eyes widened. "You know what? We probably have enough to try that, too. We could make a pattern and—"

Erin remembered now. "The stuff's red. I don't want it on my hands and feet. I'm not sure I want it on my hair, either."

"Maybe something lighter would—"

"Treena does it all the time," Cassie interrupted, "and *her* hair's not red."

Treena finished pouring the water and sat back down. Erin stared at the subtle red highlights in her blonde hair. They looked so natural. She had no idea Treena used henna. "What if it stings?" she asked Cassie, remembering the disastrous episode with the Wart Away.

"It doesn't sting, does it, Treena?"

Her older sister shook her head. "No, but if Erin doesn't want to, she doesn't want to." She took a bite from the muffin, flipped the paper open to the travel section and began to read.

Cassie ignored her. "I bought one called Midnight Plum." She stared at Erin's hair. "It's supposed to give you plummy-red highlights. Come on," she encouraged. "It's no big deal. Your hair's so dark probably no one will even notice. Just us. And Treena won't take much off the ends, will you, Treen?"

"Whatever you want, Erin." Treena frowned at her sister. "Don't be pushy. It's not your decision."

Cassie leaned close so Treena couldn't hear. "It's going to be a new you, remember?" she whispered in Erin's ear. "For the dog show. For next year." She grinned.

Erin's anger dissolved. Cassie was right. "Just how plummy is Midnight Plum, anyway?" she asked.

Cassie gave a triumphant whoop and Erin grinned. It was going to be a perfectly plummy reinvention.

"You want me to put *that* on my hair?" Erin peered at the green mud in the bowl. It looked like mushed cooked peas. Like baby food. She leaned closer and sniffed. "Eww. You've got to be kidding." It smelled like the compost pile her grandmother kept at the end of the garden.

Cassie giggled. "If it was good enough for Cleopatra, it's good enough for you." She picked up a paintbrush and dipped it in the slime. "It's not so bad. You get used to the smell after a while. Treena did."

"I don't know." Erin watched the green goop cling to the end of the brush. She was starting to have second thoughts. "Shouldn't we test it first or something?"

"Why?" Cassie poked the green slime with her fingernail. "Your mom would love this stuff. It's completely natural."

"Lots of things are completely natural but that doesn't mean I want to wear them!" Erin ran a hand through her clean, wet hair. It felt different already; Treena had taken almost two inches off the ends.

Cassie dropped the brush back into the bowl. "Sit down and put this around your neck." She handed Erin a faded pink towel. "I promise it won't sting!"

Erin sat while Cassie parted her hair with a large, silver clip. Then she began to apply the henna. Plop. Plop. Plop. She could feel the green mud hitting her hair. When Cassie began to rub it in, it felt warm and gritty.

"It feels like meat sauce or something," she complained. "Only it doesn't smell as good."

Cassie's breath tickled Erin's ear when she laughed. "Just think of it as plant sauce." She plopped another brushful of henna onto her head and began to work it in.

"I don't know about this, Cass." Erin was feeling uneasy. "The stuff's falling off." Little green spitballs of hardened henna were hitting her shoulder and dropping into her lap.

"It doesn't stick very well. Especially at first. Treena warned me about that." She pulled back and frowned at Erin. "It's not stinging your head or anything, is it?"

She shook her head. Little green balls went flying.

"Don't shake," Cassie screeched. Furiously her hands massaged Erin's head as she tried to work the henna into her hair. "A couple more minutes and we'll be done." She reached for the brush. "I promise."

It still felt gritty, Erin thought as Cassie applied the last of the henna, but it had taken so long to get it all on, that the green slime had gone from warm to cool. And though the smell made her wrinkle her nose more than once, it didn't sting one bit. It may have felt better than the Wart Away, but it took a whole lot longer to apply. After that, she had to sit with a plastic cover on her hair for an entire hour! She could hardly move. When she did, the henna fell off her head in plops and balls.

Finally, after what seemed like forever, it was time to rinse.

"Bend over more." Cassie pushed Erin's head closer to the kitchen sink.

"Owww!" She tried to lean forward. "I'm bending as much as I can."

"Maybe the bathroom would be easier," Cassie suggested as she turned on the hot water. "It's just that the kitchen sink has this great nozzle that we can move around." She pulled it out for Erin to inspect. "See?"

"This is fine." Erin stood on her toes and leaned as far forward as she could without falling over. "Let's just do it." She couldn't wait to see the color of her hair.

"Tell me how this feels." Cassie brought the nozzle to Erin's scalp.

"Hot!" she yelped.

"Sorry." Cassie adjusted the taps. "How's this?"

"Better."

They had a plan. Cassie directed the water and Erin rubbed at the henna. The plan didn't work. The henna didn't want to come out. It sat there like a green slide as the water ran off.

"Oh, no!" Erin wailed. She could see it now. She'd have little green spitballs in her hair forever. "It has to come out," she said. "It has to."

"Relax. We just need more water pressure. That's all." Cassie adjusted the taps and tried again. It didn't work.

Erin's bad feeling grew bigger. Her hair was going to be green. Gritty, globby green. Forever. "Call Treena," she ordered. "Or your mom. Call somebody." She could see it now. At the dog show. Going to school. With green hair. And it wasn't even a nice lime green. It was *slime* green.

"Treena's out," Cassie said nervously. "And Mom's working in the shop. I know. Maybe we should fill the bathtub and put you under water. For sure it'll come out then."

"No!" Sometimes Cassie could be so weird. "Get the directions," Erin instructed. "And read them out loud to me."

Cassie reached for the henna box. "'Work into the hair thoroughly.' We did that."

"Keep going."

"'Leave for an hour.'"

"Uh-huh."

"'After one hour, shampoo hair and rinse thoroughly,'" Cassie read. "'Follow with conditioner.'" She threw the box down. "I'll get my mom's shampoo and be right back." She ran from the room.

The shampoo and conditioner worked. So did the henna. Her hair was perfect, Erin decided later when she got home and stared at her reflection in her grandmother's hall mirror. Burgundy black. The color of plums. It didn't smell much like plums but she was sure that horrible green plant smell would disappear sooner or later. Besides, nobody was going to be close enough to smell it.

"Grandma!" Erin called, walking into the kitchen. She could hardly wait to see if her grandmother noticed the change. "Grandma, are you here?" There was no welcoming answer, no scramble of nails on tile as Blue rushed toward her. The house was silent. Empty.

Erin found them in the kennel. The other dogs howled their indignation as Erin walked by their cages without stopping. Her feet slowed in front of Abby's cage and, after a fast look to make sure her grandmother wasn't looking, Erin quickly tossed a dog biscuit through the bars. The Beagle pounced on it like she hadn't eaten in weeks.

"Hello, darlin'." Her grandmother didn't look up. She was on her knees in front of Duchess. Her square, capable hands were skimming the dog's stomach. "How was your afternoon with Cassie?"

"Fine." Blue came to lick her wrist and Erin scratched his head. After nosing at her pocket and finding the other dog biscuit, he wandered back to the corner to lie beside Duchess. "How is she?" Erin asked. The yellow Lab seemed to get bigger every time she saw her.

"All her vitals are good," Grandma said slowly. She was sucking on a candy; Erin saw the telltale bulge in her cheek. "And the puppies are still moving well. But I think John is right. She's probably going to be in labor in the next few days. And it's too soon."

"It's not that early, is it?"

Grandma pushed the candy from one side of her mouth to the other. "It's borderline." Worry made her voice higher than normal. "Dogs usually go into labor anywhere between fifty-nine and sixty-three days. Duchess is at fifty-seven days."

Erin tossed her head again. Her hair bounced softly against her shoulders. "That's close," she said encouragingly. She wished her grandmother would turn around.

"True. But with dogs every day counts." Grandma sighed and stood up. "I'd be happier if she'd wait at least a few more days." She turned and gave Erin a reassuring pat on the arm. "Not to worry, m'darlin'. Nature knows best. These things have a way of working out." She stared at Erin's hair and then smiled. "Very nice." She reached out to touch it. "Who cut it? Cassie?"

"Treena. Do you like the color?" She threw her head back and spread out the ends of her hair with her fingers. She caught another whiff of that plant smell. Oh, well. Suffering through that globby green slime had been worth every second.

"I think it's delightful. You've got just enough red in there to be interesting. What did you use?"

"Henna."

"Turn around," Grandma ordered. She nodded her approval when Erin turned to face her again. "Very sophisticated," she proclaimed. "It makes you look years older."

Erin grinned. Older. She looked older!

Her grandmother slipped an arm around Erin's shoulder, crunched down on her candy, and began to walk. "Come on, Blue," Grandma called. "Let's go. It's almost time for dinner." But the only part of Blue that moved was his head as he lifted it to stare at them.

"I don't think he wants to leave Duchess," Erin said.

"Fair enough." Her grandmother leaned so close that Erin could smell the minty sweetness of her breath. "When your mom sees your hair, she's going to kill me." She chuckled and gave her a squeeze. "But don't let that bother you, Erin, darlin'. It wouldn't be the first time." She laughed again, then stopped as she caught sight of a pizza delivery man. "Oh, here's our supper."

Erin watched her rush ahead to the man who waited impatiently on the steps. Grandma was great! Mom thought greasy pizza was pollution for the body, but Grandma didn't worry about stuff like that. She ordered pizza for dinner without even thinking twice about it. And she didn't flip about henna jobs either.

The smell of cheese and pepperoni carried on the wind. Erin's stomach growled as she followed Grandma inside. She walked faster. Her grandmother was cool. Cassie had said so herself. If she couldn't get tanned by showtime, she'd probably let Erin wear tights. Or even try the self-tanner. All she had to do was ask!

Chapter Ten

ERIN HAD WRITTEN Rachel several letters since arriving in Courtenay and the next afternoon she got her first response. Rachel was having a *hugely good time* at camp with the Oresti twins. Whatever *that* meant, Erin thought with a giggle as she quickly skimmed down the page. *Way cool about the dog show,* Rachel wrote. *Just think. If you win and get your picture in the paper, you can have your pick of any guy you want in grade eight.*

"I don't want a guy," Erin told Blue as they sprawled out on the grass near the kennel. "I just want a dog." The Retriever was panting softly after a long walk down by the creek.

The rest of Rachel's letter talked about camp crafts (boring), camp food (greasy), camp guys (hot), and ended with a reminder that Ridgeway Elementary rocked and grade eight ruled.

Grade eight was coming up fast. So was the dog show. Erin scratched Blue's head absently, her eyes fastened firmly on the legs that stretched out of her faded denim shorts. It had been way too hot today to wear jeans.

But that meant her skinny white legs were on display for everyone to see. Which didn't make her happy. She watched Blue chase his Frisbee. Since she'd taken Cassie's advice and "forgotten" her sunscreen, however, she couldn't very well cover herself up. Defying her mother had given her a momentary twinge. But then she'd seen Grandma's nut brown face staring at her across from the breakfast table and she'd decided that if a tan was good enough for Grandma, it was good enough for her too. No matter *what* Mom said.

A family of baby sparrows chattered noisily in the apple tree when the mother bird returned to the nest with something in her beak. Blue went to the base of the tree to see what was going on. After a minute of tail wagging and staring up into the branches, he grabbed a small stick, pranced back to Erin and laid it at her feet. His brown eyes grinned at her.

"Go for it, Blue." She threw the stick and watched the Retriever run after it. Instead of returning with his prize, he barked and playfully tossed it into the air.

Erin rolled onto her stomach and twirled a strand of hair between her fingers. She watched a tiny ant crawl up a blade of grass. Now that the green plant smell had gone, Erin loved her hair even more. John had agreed with her grandmother. The haircut and henna job made her look much older. She held out her finger and the ant traveled over it. She smiled when it fell off and disappeared into the grass. The old Erin was disappearing, too. Once she and Cassie finished the perfect reinvention, she would be a completely all new Erin Morris. Her thoughts wandered to Rachel and the start of school.

She could hear the whisper of the others as she walked into the classroom. Her hair looked like polished plums; her feet didn't trip over themselves. Her legs, her wonderfully long, smooth, tanned legs were bare and she wore only the tiniest, flippiest skirt. "There she is," they would whisper. "Erin Morris. She placed first in her dog show this summer, you know. With this incredibly gorgeous Flat-Coated Retriever called Mr. Lavender Blue. She knows everything there is to know about dogs, did you know that? She's a brain, too, that Erin Morris. Did you know? How come she wasn't on the basketball team last year? This year I think she should be captain, don't you?"

Blue's cold nose sniffed her knee and her daydream faded. School was forgotten. She giggled as Blue's rough pink tongue came out and licked her leg. All of a sudden, summer seemed so much better and she felt so much more grown up. She would be able to wear that pink skirt when she went into the ring with Blue, when she won that first place ribbon. It was all going to be perfect. She was almost perfect!

"Hello, darlin'."

Erin jumped. She had been so involved with her thoughts that she hadn't heard Grandma coming. "You scared me," she said breathlessly, looking up at her grandmother. A worried frown creased the older woman's forehead. Erin scrambled to her feet. "What's wrong?" she asked.

"Duchess's stomach has fallen," Grandma said as she and Erin walked to the house. "Her temperature is going down. The puppies will be coming soon. I've got to bring her inside and get her comfortable."

"That's okay, isn't it?" Erin held the back door open for her grandmother. "I mean she's almost at sixty days, right?" She waited until Blue was inside as well before fastening the screen behind them.

"She's at fifty-eight days," Grandma reminded her. "I'd still be happier if she waited a few more days before giving birth." She walked down the hall to the den, sank into the overstuffed green chair, wearily rubbed her eyes, and plopped her feet on a nearby crate. Duchess would whelp her puppies in the large wooden crate. And afterward, Grandma would curl up in the armchair and doze, keeping one eye on the new mother and puppies through the first night.

An uneasy feeling came over Erin as she studied her grandmother's slumped shoulders, the preoccupied look in her eyes. It wasn't the time to ask about wearing tights. She'd have to wait. "I mean, Duchess is going to be all right, isn't she, Grandma?"

Grandma sighed and smiled slightly. "I hope so, m' darlin'. Dr. Maartens was here earlier and he said everything looks fine. He'll be on standby in case there's an emergency." She glanced around the room. "In the meantime, we'd better get this place cleaned up and be ready for those pups. I want to bring Duchess into the house as soon as we can."

Erin and Grandma worked for two hours, stopping only once to pop three frozen chicken pies into the oven. Erin tidied the den while her grandmother ran a load of towels through the wash. Erin cleaned the brown heat lamp and adjusted the bulb while Grandma checked on supplies. Sensing that something important was going on, Blue refused to leave Erin's side. Even when she was almost finished and was lining the crate with old towels and a few blankets, the Retriever insisted on being in there with her.

"Out of the way, Blue." Grandma scooted the dog aside as she handed Erin a bottle of bright pink nail polish. "Put this in the corner the crate, would you, darlin'? I've got to write down Dr. Maartens emergency number."

Erin stared at the small bottle. Strawberry Ice it was called. "What's this for?" she asked.

"For the puppies," Grandma said, looking through the phone book. "To mark their toes."

"To mark their toes?" Erin frowned and put the bottle in the crate. "Why?" Blue, frustrated at the lack of attention, whined and thrust his wet nose into Erin's free hand. She gave him a scratch behind the ears. "It's okay, Blue," she whispered.

Grandma scribbled a number on a scrap of paper, tucked it beside the phone and put the book away. "I always mark the toenail of each pup." She smiled at the look of confusion on Erin's face. "That's how I can tell which is which. The first one born gets the outside left toe painted, the next gets the second from the outside left painted." She chuckled. "Sometimes they look so much alike, it's hard to remember who's who."

Excitement stirred in Erin's stomach. She laid

the last towel down and came out of the crate. Suddenly the puppies were very real to her. Very real—and arriving soon. "Do you think I can watch? I've never seen puppies being born."

Grandma slipped an arm around her shoulder. "We'll have to see how Duchess does. Usually the fewer people in the whelping room, the better." She gave Erin's shoulder a reassuring squeeze. "Mind you, if things go easily and if you're very quiet, maybe you can slip in for a little while and watch. Okay?"

"Okay," Erin agreed with a vigorous nod. Blue whined again and stuck his head between the two women. They both laughed.

"He knows something's up. He can sense it." Grandma leaned down to rub Blue's face. "Don't you, boy?" Blue's tail wagged so hard his back end swayed with the movement. "I think he smells the chicken pies, too."

At the mention of food, Erin's stomach growled. "So do I!" The savory smell of chicken and onions and pastry wafted through the air.

Grandma straightened. "Tell you what," she said. "You set the table while I go out to check on Duchess. After we eat, we'll bring her inside and settle her down."

It didn't happen quite that fast. After supper

came something Grandma called "setup time." Erin thought it was more like fussing time. Her grandmother wanted to make sure there was enough food ready for breakfast and lunch, too. In spite of Erin's assurances that she really was old enough to find the cereal and sliced meat for sandwiches, her grandmother had to make sure everything was just so.

"The leftover pizza is here, darlin'." Grandma pointed to the top shelf in the fridge where the pizza sat on a plate. "There are tins of salmon in the pantry, lots of bread in the freezer, and some chicken salad if you'd prefer that." She gestured to the plastic food saver container on the lower shelf. "And I'll put the third chicken pie down here."

Erin just nodded. Grandmothers could be as weird as parents. Why did Grandma think she was old enough to henna her hair but not old enough to figure out what to eat if she was hungry?

"I could be tied up a long time," Grandma told her again. "If you get lonely, you can always give John a call. His number is on the board beside the phone." She shut the fridge and flicked off the kitchen light. "Mind you, he'll probably be over here first thing in the morning for your training session with Blue."

The dog had been lying quietly on his blanket listening to everything Grandma said, but he jumped to attention as soon as his name was called.

"You make it sound like you're going away or something." She followed her grandmother to the back door. Blue trotted happily beside them.

"Whelpings are unpredictable and this is Duchess's first time," Peggy explained. "You stay, Blue." She shooed the black dog into the hallway and quickly shut the door behind them. "I'll probably be here the whole time but there's always a chance I might have to take Duchess over to the animal hospital. I just want you to be prepared, that's all."

The idea of being alone at her grandmother's house didn't bother Erin at all. Besides, she'd have Blue to keep her company. She could feel the Retriever's eyes on her back as she walked down the path through the garden toward the kennel. He barked in protest at being left behind.

"Can't we take him down with us?" Erin asked.

Grandma shook her head. "I don't want him all excited around Duchess. She needs quiet right now."

Instead of the barking that usually broke out when anyone approached the kennel, the other dogs were strangely subdued. It was like they knew that the birth was imminent. Even Abby simply lifted her head and wagged her tail when Erin and Grandma walked by.

Duchess was lying in a big, round lump right beside the kennel door. She was very still. Only her brown eyes moved. Slowly and solemnly they blinked.

"She looks uncomfortable," Erin observed.

"I'm sure she is." Grandma opened the door and crouched beside Duchess. "Scared, too, no doubt." Gently Grandma rubbed behind the Lab's ears. "There we go, sweetheart. It's going to be all right." Slowly her hands moved over the animal's fur, down her neck, and along her back to her stomach. There was a faraway look in her grandmother's eyes as she waited. "I can feel some tightening." She stood and studied the animal. "Probably should have moved her inside before now," she muttered. She opened the door to the kennel. "Come on, Duchess. Let's go, girl."

The animal didn't move. She just stared at Erin and Grandma like they were crazy.

"Come on, Duchess. Let's go," Erin encouraged. Large brown eyes blinked their refusal.

They tried everything to get Duchess to stand and move. Nothing worked. "Maybe we should carry her," Erin finally suggested.

Grandma shook her head. "She's too heavy. Besides, it's not a good idea with those puppies she's carrying."

"What if we bring Blue down?" Erin asked. "Maybe that'll help."

"I don't know." Grandma looked doubtful. "I don't want her excited."

Erin looked at Duchess and smiled. She felt sorry for the dog but it was almost funny the way she refused to even lift her head. "I don't think anything's going to get her really excited, Grandma." Her brown eyes blinked mournfully. "But maybe if Blue's here, she'll at least stand up."

Grandma leaned her head to one side and considered Erin's words. Finally she nodded. "Let's give it a try. Run and get Blue."

Chapter Eleven

IT WORKED. As soon as Duchess saw Blue, she not only stood but also waddled out the kennel door toward the house like she'd been waiting just for him. A few minutes later, the dog was settled in her crate and Grandma was curled up in the old green armchair beside her, a cup of milky tea in hand and an expectant smile on her face.

Erin, meanwhile, had a problem. A problem named Blue. Blue refused—absolutely—to leave the whelping room.

"Come on, Blue." She pulled on the dog's collar. "Come on!" Blue dug his feet into the old carpet and whined. Duchess, curled up on a blue blanket in a corner of the crate, studied him with her large, brown eyes.

"Why don't you take Blue and go see Cassie? Mrs. Walker told me this morning they're leaving a day early on their camping trip. Something to do with coming back early to take care of a flower order." Grandma sipped her tea. "Nothing's going to happen here for a few hours yet, and it'll keep you both busy." Her eyes remained on Duchess. "Just remember to be careful. Oh, and you might try that springer John bought you," she added.

Erin enticed Blue away from Duchess with a dog treat. Once he was outside, he trotted happily beside the bike as she pedaled down the road to Cassie's flower farm. Unfortunately, Cassie was out buying food for their camping trip. Wanting to give Blue more of a run, she decided to ride back along Dove Creek Road, past the creek and the corn fields toward the banks of Tsolum River.

It was a perfect summer night, Erin thought happily as the breeze skimmed her face. The sun was still high enough in the sky to warm her shoulders and cast shadows on the road. Blue ran contentedly beside her. Erin smiled as he tried to chase a bird— he couldn't go very far on the springer. When they reached the river, Erin glanced around to make sure they were alone. Satisfied that there was no sign of Mark or Robert, she tossed her bike on the rocks.

"*Woof!*"

She giggled and released the dog. "Okay, Blue. Go!" She reached for a stick and threw it. Blue dove into the water and searched. He surfaced without it.

His face was puzzled. He stared at her as if to ask, "What happened?"

Erin laughed out loud. "Relax," she told him. "I'll find another one." She searched the ground for the kind of stick Blue loved. He caught the second one and for several minutes the two of them played fetch and toss. After a while, Blue swam out into the river to cool off. She sat down beside her bike and watched him paddle. Soon he disappeared behind a large rock.

"Look, bro'. We have company!"

Erin jumped. It didn't sound like Mark or Robert. She turned her head and looked. It wasn't.

Two older boys smirked at her. One was tall and thin and had a cigarette dangling from his lips. The shorter one had stringy black hair and wore a ripped T-shirt. "Wanna join our party?"

"No, thanks." Erin stood up and faced them. Her palms were sweaty; she wiped them on her shorts.

"Why not?" asked the tall one. He pulled the cigarette from his lips and flicked the ashes to the ground. "We could have some fun, just the three of us."

"I don't think so." These two made Mark and Robert look like a couple of preschoolers. In spite of the warm night, she suddenly had goose bumps on her arm. Briskly she rubbed at them.

"She's got places to go, don't you, babe?" said the kid with the stringy hair. "Besides, she's a little young. And not my type." Erin flushed as he stared at her breasts, her skinny white legs. Then he kicked her bike. "Nice machine."

"I could use a bike." The tall kid's eyes narrowed as he stared at her. "How much you want for it?"

She swallowed. "It's not for sale." Hurry up, Blue, she chanted to herself. We need to get out of here. These guys are dangerous.

"Well, then, I guess I'll just have to help myself." His smirk widened to show crooked front teeth. "Kind of like a present from you to me."

The hot, sour taste of fear scalded the back of Erin's throat. With a bravery she didn't feel, she grabbed her bike and faced the two boys. "It's not for sale," she said again.

Her hands shook; she clutched the handlebars. All she had to do was wheel toward the river, find Blue, and get out. Blue. His springer. The harness. She reached for them. As she did, the kid with the stringy hair yanked the bike away from her.

"Hey!" she yelled. "Give it back!"

High-pitched laughter was their only response. "In your dreams," said the tall, skinny kid. He laughed again.

Just then Blue shot out of the water and came running. The sight of him gave her the necessary courage to reach out and grab the bike back. "It's mine," she yelled loudly. "Now get lost."

Blue raced to her side, dropped the stick from his mouth, and bared his teeth at the two boys. The hair on the back of his neck stood up like black tooth-picks. His tail was down between his back legs. Water made him shiny and slick. There was a deep, fierce growl coming from the back of his throat. He stepped a bit closer to the boys.

"Hey, man." The kid with the stringy hair held up his free hand and kept his eyes fastened on Blue. "We were only kidding, man." He laughed nervously.

"Yeah." The tall, skinny kid flicked his cigarette to the ground and slowly backed up. "Call your dog off, okay?" He fidgeted with his watch strap.

"I can't call him off," Erin lied. "He's an attack dog. If you're not out of here in two minutes flat, he'll jump you and go for your neck! You'd better get lost."

"We're going." Both boys backed up. Their eyes were big and round and they were glued to Blue. "Just keep him back, okay?"

Erin's knees were shaking now, too. She held the bike for support and stared the two boys down. "Just go," she said. "And fast."

Blue growled again and the two boys turned and ran. Blue took two steps forward and barked.

"It's okay, Blue," Erin whispered as she watched the boys scramble over the rocks and disappear into the trees. "They're gone now." She kneeled down and put her arms around the dog's neck. He was dripping wet but she didn't care. "Good boy!" she said. She scratched his ears and rubbed the top of his head. "Good, good boy!" She leaned her forehead against his. His tail lifted and began to sway. Slowly the toothpicks on his neck disappeared. He nudged Erin's hand, wanting more. When he saw the harness on the ground he pulled away and barked. A happy bark this time. A *let's go* bark.

"You may be ready but I'm not." She scanned the river for a sign of the boys. Nothing. "I need to stop shaking first." She took a couple of deep, steadying breaths. In all the years she'd come to the banks of the Tsolum River, nothing like this had ever happened before. She was going to have to be more careful. And be careful to always bring Blue with her.

She fastened Blue to the springer and began to roll the bike over the rocks. Normally she would let the Retriever run ahead, but not tonight. Tonight she wanted him as close to her side as possible.

The ride home was uneventful. By the time Erin

and Blue turned back into the driveway and strolled past the dented mailbox and the bushy holly tree, she had stopped shaking and Blue was almost completely dry. When she saw the sun setting in pink streaks between the blackened silhouettes of the fir trees and she heard the night sounds of the crickets, Erin felt almost normal again.

Blue drank long and hard from his yellow bowl, and then settled with a groan of contentment on his blanket by the stove. Erin gulped some lemonade before hurrying down the hall to Duchess and Grandma. Wait till Grandma heard how Blue had saved the day!

Her grandmother was crouched inside the crate. If she heard the door open, she paid no attention. Erin held her breath and tiptoed around the crate until she could see Duchess and her grandmother.

There was a puppy! A small tan bundle all slick and shiny with signs of birth. Her breath caught in a whistle between her teeth; her heart thudded. Thoughts of the boys by the river disappeared. It looked like a dog...but it didn't. Its eyes were shut and its whole body was curled around itself like those hermit crabs she sometimes found hiding under the rocks at the beach.

Grandma glanced up. "You're just in time," she whispered. "Puppy number one. A little girl." After

Duchess finished licking the puppy clean, Grandma gently pried open its mouth and checked the airway for mucus. Legs stretched, a tail unfurled. The puppy began to look more normal. Satisfied, Grandma cradled the small animal in her arms. "Hand me the nail polish, would you, darlin'? I've got to keep track, you know."

Duchess seemed oblivious to her presence so Erin sat quietly on the old green chair. It seemed to take forever for the next puppy to be born. Duchess moved restlessly around the crate, peering toward her behind occasionally as though she didn't understand what was happening. After a while, she began to whine. Then she stood still. Even from several feet away, Erin could see the muscles in Duchess's stomach squeeze and pull. Contractions, Grandma called them. The dog's whining got louder, deeper. Finally, after whipping her tail and hunching her back a few times like she was a camel, Duchess gave a long, deep moan. A bubble appeared. It grew bigger and then it slithered out, carrying puppy number two. It was shiny black and perfectly quiet and still.

Roughly Duchess nudged the amniotic sac and then tore at it with her teeth. Erin gasped and held her breath. Was something wrong? A puppy tumbled out in a gush of fluid, squirming and whimpering as Duchess licked and cleaned and stimulated it to life.

Erin began to breathe again. After a few minutes of attention, Duchess turned away and Grandma took over. Once the newborn was checked, Grandma held the bundle out. "It's a little boy," she said with a smile.

Her stomach flipped. Eeewww. She couldn't touch it. Not yet. "I…I can't…"

"Of course you can," Grandma insisted softly. "Take him and mark his toe. Second one from the left on his right foot," she instructed.

Gingerly, using both hands, she accepted the tiny black puppy. Her grandmother was confident enough to hold him in the palm of her hand but Erin was too nervous for that. She could feel his heart beating beneath her fingers. She stared down at him, in awe of a new life that only minutes before hadn't been.

His eyes were so tightly shut they looked like someone had sewn them closed. And though his fur was softer than Erin's white angora sweater, he wasn't nearly as pretty close up. His face was scrunched and wrinkled and his nose looked mottled and too big for his face. His front and back legs were too long for his body and they moved and stretched like limp strands of spaghetti hanging from a fork. He was altogether ugly. Helplessly, hopelessly ugly. And Erin loved him! Gumby. That's what she would call him. If he was hers to call.

"Hello, Gumby," she whispered, searching for the tiny toenail hidden in the fur. Satisfied that she'd found the right one, she carefully dabbed on bright pink Strawberry Ice nail polish. It glittered like a tiny pink ring in the black fur. Reluctant to hand Gumby back to her grandmother, she held him against her chest and gently touched her nose to the top of his soft head. He smelled like pure puppy. Her heart melted.

Her parents just had to let her have a puppy of her own. After this summer, they just had to!

When Grandma looked up, her eyes narrowed slightly at the sight of little Gumby tucked under her chin. "Someday," she said softly, guessing what thoughts were going through Erin's mind. "Someday you'll have a dog of your own to love."

It was almost midnight by the time Erin went to bed. Two more puppies had been born—both yellow —and Erin had dutifully marked their toenails with Strawberry Ice. As sweet as the animals were, none evoked the feelings she had for Gumby, the only black Lab of the litter so far. Grandma promised Erin there'd be several more puppies for her to greet in the morning and, as she dragged herself down the hall to bed, she hoped there would be at least one more black Labrador in the bunch.

There were, as it turned out the next morning, two more black Labrador puppies. Erin rubbed the sleep from her eyes and stared at them. Six puppies in all—three black and three yellow. All nursed eagerly from Duchess, who reclined on her side with resigned acceptance. Erin searched for Gumby, but it was almost impossible to tell the puppies apart. Her grandmother was right. Marking their toes with nail polish had been a good idea. One of the black puppies, however, looked larger than the others. Erin wondered if that was Gumby. Beside her, Blue gave out something that sounded like a cross between a whine and a howl.

"Shhh!" she scolded before nervously peering down the hall. There was no sign of Grandma. Maybe she had slept in her own bed, after all. "Be quiet," she ordered sternly. "You're not supposed to be in here. But just because you're a hero, I've broken the rules a bit." Blue whined his protest. Duchess thumped her tail against the newspaper. She seemed unconcerned by their presence but Erin knew her grandmother would have a fit if she caught

Blue in here disturbing the pups. Especially while they were nursing.

The back door slammed. She heard footsteps. Her grandmother! "Come on!" Hero or not, he had to go. She grabbed Blue's collar.

He dug in his heels.

Erin pulled.

He whined again, flopped on his belly, put his head on his front paws, and stared at Duchess and her babies.

"Hello, darlin'." Her grandmother's smile was bright but her pale face looked tired. "You must have just gotten up. I've only been outside a few minutes." Grandma stopped in the doorway when she caught sight of Blue. "Blue!" She put her hands on her hips. "We have a rule. No other dogs in this room."

Blue's eyes acknowledged Peggy with a blink before flicking back to Duchess and the pups. He whined again and edged forward so his black nose was touching the bottom of the crate.

Grandma sighed. "All right, Blue. You can have a few minutes. But that's it." She joined Erin and dropped a loose arm around her shoulder. "Sleep well?" she asked before turning her attention to the dogs in the crate.

Erin nodded. Except for a dream about two

headless boys who'd come tearing out of the river on huge camels, she'd slept fine. But telling her grandmother about the nightmare would take too much explaining, so she was silent. She was too interested in Duchess and her babies. Several of the puppies were finished nursing now, and Duchess was starting to clean them. Slowly and methodically her pink tongue licked their fur, gently rolling them from side to side. "It's hard to believe they grow up so quickly," she said. "When will they start to walk?"

"It won't be long. They start wobbling around even before their eyes open. At least they should." She hesitated. "I'm not sure about one of the black ones, though." Peggy chewed the corner of her lower lip.

"Why?"

"He has a problem with his left rear leg," Grandma explained. "It's twisted around in a strange way." She glanced at her watch. "I'm going to call the vet this morning. It could be a club foot. I'm not sure."

"What does that mean?"

Her grandmother hesitated. "It's not good, Erin. If it rights itself, it's fine, but if not..." Her voice trailed away.

All of a sudden, Erin's mouth was very dry. She swallowed. Not Gumby! It couldn't be Gumby.

"Which one is it?" she asked breathlessly. "Is it the one I marked?"

"No." Her grandmother shook her head. "It was the last one born. Perhaps he was squished during the pregnancy."

She tasted sweet relief. "Thank goodness," she breathed.

"Thank goodness?" Her grandmother arched her eyebrows. For once she seemed to completely misunderstand Erin. "I hardly think it's anything to be thankful for," she said tartly.

Erin flushed. "No—I mean…I thought…"

Grandma's face softened and she gave Erin's shoulders a squeeze. "I know, darlin'. I know what you meant. I'm just tired and feeling crabby. I hate getting a puppy that's not right." She propelled Erin toward the door. "It's happened twice before and I should be used to it, but it never gets any easier. Come on, Blue!" Grandma's voice sounded funny. Too high or something. "Time for breakfast." She started down the hall.

"What will you do, Grandma?"

Her grandmother was silent. She continued to walk.

"Grandma?" She asked again. "What will you do?"

Grandma stopped in the doorway of the kitchen and stared straight ahead. She picked at a button on her blouse and avoided Erin's eyes. "We'll see what the vet says, darlin'. Maybe I made a mistake. Maybe the leg will right itself in a day or two. If not, we can always try a brace. See if that helps."

"And if it doesn't?"

Grandma's eyes, when she finally did look at her, were shiny bright. "If it doesn't, we'll have to put him down. It's the only way," she said softly. "He'll have no quality of life, Erin, m'darlin'. None at all."

Chapter Twelve

"SO THEN THE VET CAME and insisted on putting the puppy to sleep," Erin told Cassie as the two girls sat on the floor in Cassie's bedroom. "But Grandma said no." Cassie had just returned from her family camping trip, so Erin was filling her in on everything that had happened during the week she was away. Between the birth of the puppies and the training sessions with Blue, the days had gone quickly. But Erin had still been anxious for Cassie to come home.

"I wanted to try the brace and Grandma agreed, even though Dr. Maartens said it was hopeless. He told Grandma to call when..." Erin lowered her voice, "when she was ready to take care of things." The words made her stomach flip all over again. "I'm exercising him every single day until he learns to walk." She stopped. "I'm calling him Twister," she whispered.

"Cool name."

"I thought so." The afternoon was sunny and hot. Even with the window wide open there was barely any breeze. But Erin couldn't appreciate the beautiful day. Poor Twister. Barely a week old. So far the exercises weren't helping much.

Cassie reached into the bowl of popcorn on the floor between them. "We had to put an animal down once." She crunched on a kernel. "When a foal was born with its kidneys outside its body. My dad and Dr. Maartens took him into the field and shot him." Unconcerned, Cassie licked her fingers. "But they didn't wait. They did it right away."

Erin gasped.

"It's for the best, really it is," Cassie added quickly when she saw the look of horror on Erin's face. "That horse should have been born dead. And those exercises may not work for Twister." She grabbed another handful of popcorn. "It would have been easier to do it right away, like the vet said. For sure before you named him."

Erin shrugged. "Maybe." The exercises would work. They had to work. Rather than ask Grandma if she could adopt Gumby, Erin had decided that Twister was the animal for her. She could give him the love he needed. She could teach him to walk.

Erin scratched Blue's head. His eyes moved back and forth from Cassie to the popcorn bowl like a Ping-Pong ball. The Retriever had come with her to Cassie's house. After her grandmother had heard about the incident at the river, she was more than willing to let Blue go anywhere with her. "My mom believes there's a reason for everything," she told Cassie. "Pain and illness even. Although she sure tries to stay healthy."

Cassie pulled on her ear cuff. "Did you talk to her about the self-tanner and stuff?"

Erin shook her head. She'd talked to her mom, but not about that.

"What about your grandma? Did you ask her about using the depilatory?"

"Nope." She hadn't thought about her legs very much since Twister had been born. "We've both been too busy. But I did *forget* my sunscreen."

Cassie stared at her legs. "It didn't help much."

"I know."

"The show's less than a week away. You have to do something."

"No, I don't." Why had she come to Cassie's anyway? Erin wondered. While her friend had been camping, she'd longed for her to come back so they could talk. Now she didn't feel like visiting. All Erin could think about was poor little Twister. And helping the dog learn to walk.

Exasperated, Cassie put the popcorn bowl down and grabbed a large purple hand mirror from under the pile of debris on her desk. She thrust the mirror under Erin's nose. "Look. You're almost perfect. Your hair's great; your eyebrows have just the right arch. You're almost there. A few more touches and the reinvention will be finished. Just in time to take Blue into the ring."

Erin just pushed the mirror aside.

"Man!" Cassie sat down on the edge of the bed with a loud sigh. "You've been a grump since you got here. What's your problem?"

Twister was the problem. If they put him down... The thought made tears prickle behind her eyes. "It's just not fair." She avoided Cassie's gaze. "About Twister."

"It wasn't fair that the foal had to die, either." Cassie tossed the mirror aside, slid from the bed to the floor, and nudged Erin with her toe. "Come on. My dad's in the business of horses and your grandma's in the business of dogs. We have to breed the best horses we can, and your grandma has to breed the best dogs she can. It makes sense when you think about it."

"It's not very nice. I think your mom has the right idea. Raise flowers instead."

"Yeah, but if they die she moans and groans like she's lost an animal or something." Cassie smiled but when Erin didn't respond with a smile of her own, she turned serious again. "Look, your grandma's trying the brace. Maybe that'll help. And I could be wrong about the exercises. Maybe they'll work, too. But worrying isn't going to help him." She picked up the popcorn and shoved it under Erin's nose. "Eat!" she ordered.

Blue whined and smacked the bowl with his right paw. Both girls giggled.

"Okay, Blue. Catch." Cassie tossed a kernel into the air and Blue caught it before it hit the ground.

Cassie was right, Erin thought. Her grandma was trying the brace. She was doing the exercises. And worrying wouldn't help Twister. Besides, she had a dog show to worry about.

"You have new hair," Cassie continued. "And new eyebrows. Not only that, I'm sure the spell's working because your warts are starting to shrivel. I'll bet if we dug up that garlic, it would be rotting in the ground as we speak."

Erin studied her hand. The warts did seem a little bit smaller. Especially the older one.

"All that's left of the perfect reinvention is your legs," Cassie said. "You could ask your grandmother about wearing tights. But in this heat, she'd probably want your legs left bare. And even if she said yes, you'd look pretty stupid wearing them."

Erin's thought exactly. Her hair swung forward as she dipped into the popcorn bowl.

"You could ask your grandma about using a depilatory but she might say no. Especially since your mother already has."

Erin had thought about that, too.

"I say go ahead and use the stuff and suck up the consequences later. For the sake of being the best you can be. For the sake of *winning*."

For the sake of winning. For being the best she could be. Sheila Jones had said being the best was important, and she should know. She'd been a judge once.

Erin was pretty close to being her best self now. She had new hair; her warts were getting smaller. Did her legs really matter? She thought about the girls at the bakery, the boys at the river, all the nasty whispers she'd endured in gym class in the last year. In the ring, people would stare. That's what they did. And if everything *but* her legs was fixed, that might work against her. Erin couldn't let anything stand in the way of winning. It wasn't just her pride at stake. Blue's win mattered to Grandma, too. Her mother would have to understand.

"Okay," she said. "Bring out everything you've got."

Cassie let out a hoot of excitement. "Yes!" she said triumphantly. The popcorn went flying to the floor and Blue scrambled to clean up.

"I don't know about this, Cassie. It just doesn't feel right." Erin was balanced on the bathroom vanity, wedged between the sink and the door, with her feet propped up on the edge of Cassie's bathtub. She peered at her legs. All she could see was white hair removal foam. Gobs and gobs of it from her knees to her ankles. She couldn't decide if it smelled more like rubber boots or a really stinky perfume. It just smelled awful. And it felt a whole lot worse. "It's burning," she said nervously. "Like acid or something."

"Whoever said being beautiful was easy?" Cassie asked brightly. She was perched on the toilet painting her toenails with polish called Hot Cocoa. Blue was crammed against the bathtub, his brown eyes fastened firmly on Erin.

"It just doesn't feel right." She jumped down from the vanity, suddenly sure that she didn't want this white foam on her legs anymore. "I want to wash it off. Right now." Blue nudged her leg with his cold nose. A streak of the cream covered his head. "No, Blue!" She wiped the cream from his fur. The sting was getting worse.

"But we read the directions. And it said we have to keep it on for fifteen minutes." Cassie glanced at the red timer ticking away on the counter. "We still have six minutes to go."

"It also said to test it on your skin first, remember?" Erin reminded her friend. "In case you're allergic or something." Her legs were burning up. They felt like they were on fire. "I think I'm allergic, Cassie. I'm allergic to cats. I'm probably allergic to this hair remover stuff, too." Now it was starting to itch. A hot, burning itch that was worse than anything she'd ever felt in her life. "Run the water, Cassie. I'm taking this stuff off right now!"

Blue stood up and began to whine.

"Now!"

Cassie jumped up. Her nail polish fell to the floor and Hot Cocoa dribbled out. "Oh, no!" she cried, staring at the mess. "Mom's going to kill me."

"Never mind!" Erin cried back. "We'll clean it up later. Just turn on the water." Blue whined and tried to wrap himself around Erin's right leg, covering one side of his fur with the white leg cream as he went.

"Hurry up," Erin said nervously. "Now it's on Blue. We have to rinse him off, too." Tears gathered behind her eyes.

Cassie turned on the tap. Erin jumped into the bathtub, stuck her legs under the water and scrubbed furiously with the brown washcloth Cassie handed her. Slowly the water dissolved the foam and eased the itch, but her leg still burned. "Get Blue in the tub too, Cass. We have to clean him off."

"I can't do that! I'm already going to be in trouble for this!" Cassie was wiping up the nail polish on the floor.

"Well, that's nothing compared to the trouble I'll be in if Blue goes bald!" Erin blinked hard to stop the tears from falling. "Grandma will kill me. And I can't take a bald dog into the dog ring. We have to wash him!"

"Okay."

The two girls hoisted the animal into the tub. Blue thought it was a game. He stood still while they cleaned him off but then he started to jump and prance and play with the brown loofah hanging from the shower shelf. Cassie forgot her fears and thought it was all very funny.

Erin didn't.

Her legs were still burning up. She was scared to look at them. What if she'd wrecked them forever? What if she'd permanently damaged her skin? Cassie had promised her the cream was safe. Maybe she was just having an allergic reaction. Blue shook and droplets of water landed in Erin's eyes. Cassie giggled again but Erin failed to see the humor in the situation. "I'm getting him out now," she told Cassie. "Do you have a towel I can use to dry him off?"

"I'll dry him," Cassie said. "You sit on the edge of the tub and towel off."

While she did, Erin watched Cassie dry Blue with an oversized beach towel. Blue lapped up the attention. He even kissed Cassie on the cheek. *Dear God of Dogdom*, Erin prayed silently, *don't let him go bald.*

"There," Cassie said as she gave Blue one last rub, "as good as new." She threw the towel into the hamper and was about to let Blue out of the bathroom when her eyes landed on the bathtub. "Look," she said, pointing to the bottom of the tub. "It started to work." She reached over and shut off the tap. Blue rested his head on the edge of the tub and wagged his tail.

Erin's eyes followed Cassie's finger. Traces of foamy white cream flecked with black floated toward the drain. The cream had worked!

She pulled the towel from her legs and stared. For a minute nothing made sense. But when she realized what she was looking at, Erin felt sick to her stomach. "Oh no!" The cream had taken away patches of hair, leaving the rest looking like twisted mini pretzels. What was she going to do?

Cassie studied Erin's legs. "It looks like a chessboard," she finally said, "with those patches of white skin and the dark hair that's left. Very punkish. Somebody would probably pay to have that done." She grabbed some paper towels from under the sink and finished cleaning up the spilled nail polish.

"We have to do something!" Grandma was going to have a fit. "I can't go into the ring like *this*."

There was a loud tap on the bathroom door. "You girls all right in there?" It was Cassie's mother.

"Fine!" Cassie yelled back. She threw the soiled towels in the trash.

Blue woofed twice.

Erin wiped her tears away. "We're not fine," she hissed. "At least I'm not. My legs are burning up."

"I know, I know." Cassie looked worried, too. "But look, the hair's almost gone. We'll shave away the rest. Then use the self-tanner. That should take away the sting."

"Quit squirming," Cassie ordered.

"I'm trying not to," Erin said. But her legs itched. She leaned back in the bedroom chair, kept her legs firmly propped up on the desk, and watched Cassie apply the shiny black lotion. It looked like something you would stain furniture with. "Are you sure it's okay to use this tanning stuff after shaving?"

"Positive." Cassie went to work on her lower left leg. "I do it all the time. And this tanner and bronzer in one is my favorite. It's nice and dark, which means you can't miss a spot when you put it on."

"My legs are still itching," Erin said. Over in the corner, Blue dozed, his eyes twitching in a happy little dream.

"Give it a few minutes. It's not dry yet. Just think— three or four hours from now you'll have an allover instant tan." She went to work on Erin's right leg.

Erin bit her lip and ignored the itching. It wasn't that bad. She was just being paranoid.

"Done," Cassie said a few minutes later. "I'll go wash my hands." She gestured to one of Treena's old *In Style* magazines. "You can read that while you're waiting."

By the time Cassie got back from the bathroom, the itching had turned into a hot burn. "It hurts, Cass. Really."

"You are such a wuss." Cassie flopped onto her bed and picked up a horse magazine. "It can't be that bad."

Two minutes later, Erin threw the magazine down. "It *is* that bad. It feels like my legs are on *fire.*"

Cassie looked up, sighed. "Okay, okay. I'll go get the fan. Maybe some air will help."

"No." Erin jumped up from the chair. "I'm washing it off." She threw open Cassie's bedroom door and ran down the hall to the bathroom.

"You're not supposed to get your legs wet for an

hour," Cassie said, hurrying after her. "You could mess the whole thing up."

"I don't care." Erin was already in the bathtub running the water. "This much pain can't be normal." She splashed cool water on her legs. Instant relief. "Hand me a washcloth, Cass." Her friend hesitated. "Seriously," Erin said. "Or I'll use this." She gestured to the bath towel hanging on the rail.

Wordlessly, Cassie handed her a brown washcloth. A few minutes later, Erin was done. Signs of the tanner-bronzer were gone. But ugly streaks of orange ran the length of Erin's legs. And welts the size of quarters were beginning to form.

Panic turned Erin's stomach inside out. What was she going to do?

"I'm so sorry," Cass whispered as she followed Erin back to the bedroom. "I use the tanner all the time and my mom uses the cream all the time and we never have any problems."

The two girls sat on the bed. Erin stared at her legs. Was it her imagination or were more welts forming before her eyes? "I knew we should have tested that stuff first."

It was too late now.

There was a whimper from the corner of the bedroom. Blue was dreaming. Erin watched the dog's ears twitch and his eyelids move. He whined again. Erin had a sudden vision of a bald Blue or worse, a half-bald Blue with tufts of twisted pretzel hair where his fur used to be. "Oh man," she breathed. "If that cream did this to me, Blue could be in real trouble."

A look of horror crossed Cassie's face; she quickly recovered. "You don't know if it was the hair stuff. It could've been the self-tanner."

"Maybe. But I can't go into the ring looking like this. And if Blue goes bald..." She stopped. "I have to tell Grandma." She studied Blue's side. It looked normal. So far.

"I'll come with you," Cassie offered bravely.

Erin shook her head. "No. I'll do it myself."

"Are you sure?" she asked.

She wanted Cassie to come, but her parents always talked about being responsible for your actions. She figured this was one of those times she had to be responsible, no matter how much trouble she got in.

"I'm sure." Her mouth stung like bitter lemon. It was the taste of worry. She swallowed, hoping to chase it away. "It'll be fine," she said firmly.

It *had* to be fine.

Chapter Thirteen

"**H**AVE ANOTHER PIECE OF CHICKEN, DARLIN'."
Grandma held the platter under Erin's nose. Blue,
lying quietly on his bed, followed the platter of
chicken with his eyes.

Politely, Erin shook her head. She shifted her legs
again and tried to resist the urge to scratch. She lost.
For the one hundredth time since she had sat down
to dinner, her fingers reached under the table.
Scratch, scratch, scratch. It was the absolute worst
itch she'd ever had. She should have told Grandma
as soon as she came home. Instead, she'd been so
scared, she'd put it off. She would tell her after dinner, Erin vowed. For sure.

Grandma helped herself to a chicken leg and put
the platter down. "I'm still not sure what to do about
that pup." She spooned carrots out of the bowl and
placed them beside the chicken. "Dr. Maartens was
here again. He thinks it's time to put him down."

Erin's fingers stopped mid-scratch. Not yet!

Twister would be fine. She would exercise him until he walked. Until he ran!

Grandma sighed and stared blankly at the food on her plate. "I'm just not sure," she said again.

Erin had been sure when she'd come home from Cassie's house that her grandmother would know something was wrong. That would have made it easier to tell her. But Grandma hadn't noticed Erin's mad rush to the bedroom to grab some jeans, nor had she said anything about her granddaughter's continual scratching.

"What about the brace?" Erin's legs were itchy again. This time she wouldn't scratch. She *wouldn't*.

"Dr. Maartens says it's not working." Grandma pushed her chicken leg around the plate. "It could take some time, and with the way the other dogs are picking on him—"

"Picking on him? On Twister?" All of a sudden Erin was ashamed of herself. Her problem seemed small compared to what Twister was facing.

"Twister?"

Erin flushed. "That's what I've been calling him."

"Don't name him, darlin'." Grandma's eyes were gentle. "Not this one."

Of course he needed a name. All dogs needed a name. Unless… Erin swallowed the lump in her

169

throat. "What do you mean, they're picking on him?" She wouldn't think about the "unless" part.

"It happens, Erin. It's survival of the fittest. All animals do it. It usually happens to the smallest one. In this case, it's the one with the bad leg."

"Maybe you should take him out of the litter, then." She rubbed at her left leg. Rubbing didn't count. It wasn't scratching.

"He needs his mother for another week at least," Grandma explained. "I guess I could pull him out of the crate and just put him back for feedings, but I don't feel right about it. The poor thing is so listless and sad. He just lies in the corner. He doesn't seem to want to live. Maybe Dr. Maartens is right," she mused. "Maybe it's time to make a decision."

"Wait a few more days. I'm doing these exercises with him and I know they're going to work. He's going to make someone a perfect pet!" Like me, Erin added silently.

"We'll see." Grandma pushed her uneaten chicken away and methodically wiped her fingers on a napkin. "Now," she said, her brown eyes fastened firmly on Erin's face, "just what is the problem with your legs, m'darlin'?"

Erin felt the flush start at her neck and travel up past her forehead to the roots of her hair. "I…ah…"

She dropped her eyes to the table. How could she tell her grandmother what she'd done to herself—to Blue?

"What kind of trouble did you and Cassie concoct this time?" Grandma asked. There was an easy smile on her face.

"I have this rash," Erin began cautiously, "on my legs."

"And how did that come about?"

"Oh, Grandma, it's just awful!" She fought back tears. "Mom doesn't want me to have a tan—you know how she is about sunscreen—and my legs are so white it makes all the hair stand out even with shaving and I get teased and now I have to wear a skirt in the ring with Blue so Cassie and I decided to do this reinvention to make me look better and we used this hair-removal cream plus this self-tanner stuff but I think I had an allergic reaction and now I'm covered with horrible red marks." The words poured out of Erin. "And when we were washing off the hair-removal stuff, Blue brushed up against my leg and smeared it all over his fur so now I'm afraid he'll be bald which would be horrible for a dog and especially one in a dog show!" Erin was out of breath by the time she finished speaking.

"I see." A small smile hovered on her grandmother's lips. "So you used a depilatory."

Erin nodded. "And a self-tanner."

"And how long did Blue have the depilatory on?"

"Not long. Less than a minute. Way less. We washed it off right away."

Grandma's smile deepened. "He'll be fine, Erin. He has a thick coat. It probably didn't touch the roots. Don't worry about him."

In spite of her grandmother's reassurance, Erin's eyes sought out the spot on Blue's side. It looked perfectly, wonderfully, normal. If only it stayed that way.

"What about you?" Grandma asked. "Did you test the cream on your skin first?"

"*No!*" Erin wailed. "And I told Cassie we should have, but you know what Cassie is like."

Grandma pushed her chair back from the table. "Let's see," she said briskly.

Erin spun around, lifted her legs onto her grandmother's knees. Blue, sensing that dinner was over, inched his way forward toward the table, his ears at attention, his eyes focused on the few pieces of chicken remaining on the platter.

"Blanket, Blue," Grandma ordered without even looking up. Gently her fingers rolled up Erin's jeans.

Her skin was a patchwork of big red welts and streaks of orange. Just looking at it made Erin feel sick to her stomach all over again.

Her grandmother ran two fingers over one leg. "That's quite the reaction," she murmured. "If it's any consolation at all, my dear, you come by it honestly." She raised her head and gave Erin a sympathetic smile.

"I do?"

"Mmm hmm." Her grandmother nodded before looking back at the leg. "Had the same reaction to depilatories myself, only I did a skin test on my wrist first. Broke out in horrible welts. Never went near the stuff again."

"What did you do?" Erin demanded.

"I waited it out."

"I don't have time to wait! What can I do?" She started to scratch, but Grandma stopped her.

"Leave it be," she ordered mildly. "Don't aggravate it any more than it already is." She pulled Erin's jeans down and lowered her legs to the floor. "A good long soak in Epsom salts will relieve the itch." Grandma stood up. "The redness will take a few days to fade, I'll wager. But you should be fine by showtime. If not, you can always wear tights."

Relief waterfalled through her. So what if it ended up being a hot day. It was better than the alternative. But reality quickly intruded. "I'll still have skinny white legs." A lone tear snaked its way down her cheek. "Even when I shave them they look ugly." Another tear escaped and Erin wiped at her face with the back of her hand.

"Because the hair grows back so fast?"

"Exactly. So I wear jeans all the time, except in gym when I have to wear shorts, and you should hear what some of the guys say. They're really mean."

Grandma sighed. "You might have to wax."

"But that *hurts.*"

"No pain, no gain." She smiled. "Besides, after a few years the roots weaken and the hair doesn't grow in as thick." She stared at Erin's legs. "And a bit of a tan wouldn't hurt either."

"Tell me about it," Erin muttered. "Mom packed, like, two gallons of sunscreen and insisted I use it."

"I love your mother dearly—you know that—but she can be a little obsessive," Grandma said. "One doctor in Boston believes too much sunscreen can be a dangerous thing. And some sun can be good for you. Vitamin D and all that."

"She says I can take cod liver oil instead."

Grandma snorted. "How lucky for you."

Erin giggled through her tears.

"Have you told your mother what the other kids are saying?"

After blowing her nose, Erin nodded. "She doesn't get it. She thinks I'm exaggerating and that it's not so bad. Her legs are short, mine are really long. They stand out more. Plus, the hair on her legs is so blonde you can hardly see it, you know?"

"Oh, I know," Grandma replied.

Erin looked closely at her grandmother. "You do?"

"The kids teased me, too. All the time. And in those days, girls didn't wear pants to school."

"What did you do?"

"Suffer mostly," her grandmother replied. "Wear thick tights and fight with my mother about shaving my legs." She chuckled. "They didn't have depilatories in those days, either, so I mixed sugar and water to a paste and pulled the hair off. It was torture and my mother and father were furious but it was worth it." She chuckled again. "I was pretty near your age, too."

Hope spread through Erin like a shaft of sunlight entering a darkened room. Her grandmother understood.

"I'll talk to your mother," Grandma said. "See if I can convince her to let you get a little bit of color on your legs. We might need to use a bit more self-tanner to even out the tan once the welts go down." She stood and pulled Erin to her feet. "In the meantime, into the bath with you."

"The self-tanner would be great." Erin followed her grandmother down the hall. "Especially if I could use it all year long and it would hide my knobby knees and make my legs look way better. I'd be a whole new perfect me."

"You're perfect now, Erin," her grandmother said as she pulled a bag of Epsom salts from the hall cupboard. "A little bit of a tan on your legs will change things less than you think."

Erin was usually slow to wake up in the morning. Gradually the sound of birdsong would filter through her brain. Gradually she would be aware of Blue wheezing softly on his pillow beside the bed. Then she would stretch and think about breakfast, about what she had planned for the day.

Wednesday she was instantly awake.

Something was different.

Blue was on his pillow, wheezing softly. And he had all his hair, so it wasn't that.

Erin stretched and tried to remember what was different. Then she knew. Her legs were different. They were smooth and slick. Erin rubbed them together a second time. Slip, slide. She grinned. The welts were almost gone. And the depilatory had taken away the awful stubble.

Grandma had finally gotten through to her mom, too. Erin wasn't sure what Grandma had said—she had taken the phone call in her bedroom. But after a while Grandma had come to fetch her and Erin had gotten on the phone herself. Her mother had been very quiet, the way she was when she was upset, only Erin couldn't figure out what it was her mother had to be upset about. It was her leg problem. Anyway, her mother had told Erin in her quiet voice that if the problem was so serious that it was ruining her life, she could get a light tan. As long as she didn't burn. And stayed out of the sun between twelve and two. She could use the self-tanner once more, to even out the streaks. But her mom certainly didn't want her using it all the time. At least not until she looked into it more thoroughly.

Erin had nodded into the phone, swallowed the whoop of joy in her throat, and told her mother several times that her life would be *way* better if she was tanned. For sure, her legs would look better. And probably the rest of her, too.

It had been as easy as that.

Afterward, Erin and Grandma had celebrated with root beer floats on the back patio. It was the best present her grandmother had ever given her, and Erin told her so.

She jumped out of bed and examined her legs. The blotches were fading. With a few more Epsom salts baths and some sun, they should be completely gone by the weekend. By show day.

Blue stretched on his pillow and opened his mouth wide in an early morning yawn.

"Just a minute, Blue. I have to get dressed first." Automatically Erin reached for jeans, but her hand stopped midair when realization struck. Instead she pulled on denim capris and a gray Nike T-shirt. She grinned at herself in the mirror. No more hiding her legs!

Her grandmother was wrong, Erin decided as she padded down the hall toward the back door to let Blue out. Having smooth legs had changed things. Just wait till she used the self-tanner to even out the streaks. It would be the best. She touched the warts on her hand. They were almost gone, too. The reinvention was almost done. Soon she would be perfect.

There was a note on the kitchen counter propped against some apple Danishes. "Gone to see Sheila Jones," Erin read out loud. "Will be back by ten-thirty. Remember, John comes at ten." Erin glanced at the clock. It was just after nine. She had an hour to eat and exercise Twister.

She put some food in Blue's dish and refreshed his water. She glanced out the window to see if the dog was ready to come in, but he was busy sniffing down by the apple tree. It was a nice morning. He would be outside for a while. She poured herself a large glass of orange juice, picked through the Danishes to find two with the most icing, and headed down the hall to the puppies.

"Okay, guys, okay!" Erin giggled as the puppies wobbled over to greet her. Her parents would be arriving for the dog show in just a few days and she couldn't wait for them to see the pups! She was sure they'd love them as much as she did. The little bundles of fur tumbled and fell over each other in their enthusiasm to get to Erin.

"In a few minutes." She sat down in the old green chair and took a bite out of a Danish. "Let me eat my breakfast first." She knew from experience that if she let the pups out now, they'd be all over her. And her breakfast. Grandma had just started introducing solid food. Apple Danishes weren't on their menu. Instead they got plain old baby Pablum mixed with a little yogurt. It looked gross but the puppies loved it.

The pups were still really young but Erin was sure she could already tell their personalities apart.

There was Gumby, prancing and playing with one of the yellow puppies. Gumby, Erin decided, was a playful tease who liked to roughhouse. He was playing with a dog Erin called Honey. Honey was a sweet-natured female who loved to cuddle and lick.

She wiped the crumbs from her fingers, took a long gulp of orange juice, and went to work on her second Danish. She watched Gumby try to wrestle with Honey, but the dogs were still a little young for that. Soon another stocky yellow waddled over. Erin called him Arnold, after the Terminator. A fat black puppy began to bark. "You tell 'em, Fred," Erin said. That one reminded her of Fred Flintstone. He was the loudest of the bunch. Over in the corner was the first-born puppy Grandma laughingly called The Snob because she rarely joined in with the others. Erin thought she had the prettiest face of them all. She called her Mercedes, after the car.

And, of course there was Twister.

Where *was* Twister?

Quickly Erin scanned the crate. She couldn't see him. Maybe he was nursing? But Duchess was sitting on her haunches watching her puppies with a big Mama grin on her face. Erin could see her belly clearly. There was no nursing puppy there.

The Danish stuck in Erin's throat. She stopped

chewing. No! It couldn't be. She put the Danish down and forced herself to take a long, deep breath before her eyes slowly scanned the crate again. Twister had to be there somewhere.

Chapter Fourteen

THERE HE WAS! In the corner, almost covered by the old gray blanket. Sleeping soundly. She could see the brace clearly now. It looked like two padded Popsicle sticks taped together. Her heart stopped pounding. She picked up her Danish and resumed chewing. For a minute she'd thought her grandmother had taken him away! But Twister was still there.

She licked her fingers and stood. "Get up, little guy," she said softly. "It's exercise time." The other puppies rushed at her. Twister still slept. "Okay!" She laughed as the puppies scrambled and fell over each other in their haste to get to the edge of the crate. "I'll play with you first."

After she finished with the other puppies, Blue barked to come inside. She let him in and returned to the crate. Twister was still asleep. Erin leaned down, gently removed the blanket, and picked him up. He was a small ball of soft black fur. She cupped him under her chin and carried him to the old red blanket in the corner. "Let's see what you can do today," she murmured into his ear.

Twister yawned and stretched before giving her finger a gentle lick with his tiny, pink tongue. She smiled. But when she placed Twister on the ground, his legs wouldn't support his weight. He fell over. Her smile disappeared.

"Come on, sweetie," she coaxed. "Stand up." She slipped her fingers under Twister's belly and forced him up. The leg with the brace stood at attention, but his three other legs folded under him. When she let go, Twister curled into a ball and lay his head on the blanket. "You're going to have to work extra hard today, Twister. The show's coming up and I'm going to be busy for a few days." She went to work on Twister's legs. She had the routine down pat by now. Massage, bend, stretch. Massage, bend, stretch. Every few minutes she stopped the routine and encouraged the puppy to stand.

Twister always fell back with a soft plop.

"Come on, Twister," she encouraged. "Just try." She frowned. Was it her imagination or was Twister worse today? Blue came in to see what she was doing, but Erin shooed him away. Massage, bend, stretch. Massage, bend, stretch.

"Erin?" John's voice traveled down the hall.

"Hi, John," she yelled back. She glanced at her watch. Yikes! An hour had passed. Once again she tried to get Twister to stand. Once again the puppy's legs wouldn't support his weight.

"Somehow I thought I might find you in here." John stood in the doorway, watching. "How's it going?"

"Good!" She made the word come out firm and strong. "Come on, Twister," she whispered. "Stand."

As soon as her fingers released him, the puppy's legs folded beneath him. His tiny head hit the blanket with a gentle plop.

"Doesn't look so good to me," John said.

"We just need to work on it some more," she said. "That's all."

John glanced at his watch. "Time's up for today, I'm afraid. Ready to go?"

She gave Twister a quick cuddle under her chin before lowering him into the crate. She made sure she left him as she found him, in the corner with the gray blanket tucked around him for comfort. "I should probably change." Her capris covered most of the blotches and streaking but not all of it.

"You look fine," John said. "It's a casual day. They're setting up the field, remember? But it's a great opportunity to get Blue used to the site before the show."

Erin took one last look at Twister before she left the room. "He just needs exercise, you know," she told John again. "He's going to be fine!"

"We'll talk in the car," he said.

He didn't believe her! Erin opened her mouth to argue but John was already out the door. Blue, knowing a car ride was just seconds away, was right behind him. She grabbed the dog's leash from the kitchen drawer, followed John to his Jeep and slid into the passenger seat. Blue wedged himself between Erin and John and stared happily out the window. Blue loved going in the car almost as much as he loved running beside Erin's bike.

"It's true, you know," she said when they were on their way. "Twister will walk. I'll make him!"

"It doesn't work that way, Erin." Blue's head was in the way and she couldn't see John's face, but he sounded sad. "There's a certain standard—"

"Of perfection," she interrupted hotly. "I know all about it."

The light up ahead turned green and John stepped on the gas. "There's that, yes, but what I was going to say was that there's a certain standard of life," John explained mildly. "That puppy will probably never walk. He'd have to be carried all the time. What kind of life is that for a dog?"

When Erin was silent, John reached out and gave Blue's head a scratch. "Look at this guy. He's full of spit and vinegar. He can't wait to get up in the morning and chase birds or bring you a stick. He'd be miserable if he couldn't do it."

"Twister will chase birds one day, too!" Erin vowed swiftly. "*And* bring sticks."

"Maybe," John replied softly. "And maybe not."

Blue was panting from the heat in the Jeep and Erin rolled down her window. Adults didn't understand anything!

"The fact is, Erin, your grandma has a business to run," John continued. "And sometimes that means making hard decisions. Don't expect too much of her."

The only thing Erin expected was that Twister would walk. He would!

John pulled into the parking lot at the Comox Valley Exhibition Grounds. "Looks like other people had the same idea." There were half a dozen cars and trucks scattered about. Erin watched an older woman carefully remove a pampered-looking Cocker Spaniel from the back of a blue sedan. Across the field she could see several men raising poles and tents. The door to the hall was open; animals and people were moving around inside.

The dog show was only three days away and she was going to be part of it! Erin's stomach flip-flopped. "Come on, Blue." She fastened the leash around the Retriever's neck. "Be on your best behavior." She opened the door to the Jeep and jumped down.

"Remember, Blue hasn't done this for a while," John reminded her as they headed in the direction of the hall. "He's bound to be excited."

A Welsh Corgi barked a greeting as they went inside. Blue barked back. Erin grinned. John frowned. Immediately she jerked on Blue's leash. "Quiet, Blue," she reprimanded him.

John nodded approvingly. "Good. Show him who's boss." He pointed to a table against the far wall. "We'll pick up the schedule before we check out the field."

The hall smelled like sneakers and sweat and old gym clothes. Of gym class. Erin's heart thudded. She hated gym class.

Don't go there.

"John! How are you?" A lady in a large flowery dress waddled out from behind the table. A big black Bouvier followed her. Erin could feel Blue straining to get close to the other dog, so she leaned close to his ear. "Settle, Blue," she whispered.

"This must be Peggy's granddaughter." The woman had a voice bigger than her dress. "I'm Melissa McClanahan. But you can call me Missy. Everyone else does." Her wide face stretched into a fat grin and she held out her hand. The big black Bouvier opened his mouth in a giant yawn.

Erin fought back a giggle. "Hello." Politely she shook the woman's hand. "I'm Erin."

"Well now, Erin, here's your schedule," Missy practically shouted as she handed Erin a large beige envelope. You're on at noon. Nevertheless, I suggest you look everything over thoroughly just in case you have questions." Her voice echoed around the gym. "I'm the person to ask, you know." The Bouvier yawned again and this time Erin did giggle.

"Now I know you're nervous." Missy yelled. "But don't let that worry you. Everyone's nervous. My granddaughter will be showing in the same class as you. I'll make sure the two of you meet."

Maybe she couldn't hear very well, Erin thought, although she didn't see a hearing aid. "Don't forget to bring a dog crate," Missy instructed. "He seems well behaved, but of course you never know what they'll do on show day. It's always good to have somewhere to put them if they start to get excited."

The Bouvier made a sound that was a cross between a huff and a sneeze.

"Oh, Alberto. Bless you, darling."

Alberto lay down with a groan. Blue took a few steps forward and the two dogs sniffed noses.

Erin smirked at John. Alberto? Sounded like somebody in a hair commercial.

John hid his smile. "And how is Alberto these days?" he asked. "Last time I saw him, he had a bad hip."

The heavy-set woman gave the Bouvier an indulgent smile. "He recovered nicely—didn't you, darling?" She gazed around the hall impatiently. "Veronica! Over here, Veronica." As Missy waved, the flowers on her dress danced up and down. "You'll get to meet my granddaughter after all," she beamed.

"Hello, Grandmother."

Erin recognized the voice. Her stomach sank to her toes. Maybe she was wrong. Slowly she turned. Her stomach fell out the end of her shoes. Just her luck!

It was the girl from the bakery. The girl with the purple streak in her hair and the neck like a giraffe.

"This is Veronica." Missy threw her arms around the girl and gave her a hug. "And Sugar, of course."

She patted the golden Pomeranian under Veronica's arm. "You girls must be close to the same age. How wonderful that you'll have each other to spend time with."

Erin would rather stick needles in her eyes than spend time with *her*.

Veronica nodded as if she'd never seen Erin in her life. "Hello." She played with the pale pink bow attached to her dog's fur. "It's nice to meet you." The coolness in her tone suggested otherwise. Her gaze fastened on the bits of Erin's legs visible in her capris. Just then, Blue wandered out from behind the table. "Nice…," Veronica hesitated, "dog." Her grin was smirky, mean.

Why hadn't she thrown on jeans before leaving Grandma's house? "Thank you." It was Erin's turn to feign politeness.

"*Eii, eii, eii, eii, eii!*" Sugar the Pomeranian caught sight of Blue. She put back her ears and howled. Blue wagged his tail and walked toward her. "*Eii, eii, eii,*" the Pomeranian howled louder. Blue stopped, put back his ears, and whined.

Veronica shushed her dog. Erin grinned. Sugar wasn't shushing.

"Now, now, Sugar," Missy fussed loudly. "It's all right, sweetheart." Blue whined a second time.

Alberto merely yawned. A few of the other dogs in the hall, however, began to bark. Missy frowned. "Give her a biscuit, Veronica, darling. That always settles her down."

Veronica reached into the pocket of her black Nike track suit, pulled out a pale green dog biscuit, and shoved it under Sugar's nose. "*Eii, eii, eii, eii.*" Sugar twisted like a knot in Veronica's arms. She didn't want a biscuit. Veronica struggled to hold onto the dog. The dog bone dropped. So did the pale pink bow in Sugar's hair. Blue ambled over, sniffed the bow, and promptly ate the dog bone.

Erin and John laughed.

"*Eii, eii, eii, eii, eii.*" Sugar didn't like that at all. She clawed her way up to Veronica's shoulder and jumped. Her nails clicked against the floor as she ran for freedom.

Veronica turned the color of a radish and ran after her.

Missy's smile was apologetic. "Veronica is so good with her but these little dogs can be high-strung sometimes."

Erin snorted.

"Bless you," Missy said distractedly.

"Yes, well...we must be off, too," John said, steering Erin and Blue toward the door.

"Good luck," Missy yelled after them. "Once Sugar gets used to Blue, I'm sure you and Veronica will become fast friends."

In your dreams, Erin thought. Instead she smiled and nodded.

Outside, dogs and owners wandered around like they were out for a casual walk through the park. All except Sugar, who was now making *eii, eii* noises at a German Shepherd.

"Heel, Blue." Erin made sure Blue was in perfect form as he trotted by the high-strung Sugar. She gave Veronica a wide, sunny smile. She was rewarded with a sulky look.

"It'll look different on Sunday," John said. He pointed to the middle of the field, where an official with a clipboard measured the ground with a tape measure. "That man is figuring out where the ring will go." John turned and gestured to the side of the field. "The judge will be about there, and the ring will be in front. You'll enter from somewhere back here and go through your paces. Blue will always be between you and the judge. There will be tables for the smaller dogs to pose on and the kennel area too, of course."

A few birds scratched in the grass nearby, and Blue strained against the leash. He wanted to run. Erin released him. The birds scattered as the dog chased them. "I don't think we need to worry about the kennel area," Erin said. "Blue's pretty obedient." She called and he ran back to her. "See?"

John leaned down and scratched Blue's ears. "He's a good dog, there's no question. But it can be pretty crazy around here on show day. The crate will give him somewhere to be quiet." He straightened. "Now let's find a place and put Blue through his paces."

They worked Blue for about twenty minutes before letting him go off and familiarize himself with all the strange smells. Some of the other owners followed suit, and soon a small group of dogs wandered happily across the grass. Even Sugar stopped making those horrible *eii, eii* noises though she really wasn't very good at following commands, preferring to bark cheekily every time Veronica issued one. By the time they headed for home, Erin felt confident and excited.

"I think he's going to win," she told John as he drove past the Walker flower farm.

"Don't count your eggs before they're hatched," John said with a chuckle. "Blue's good but so are lots of other dogs."

"Blue's the best." Erin reached out to give the dog a hug. She was rewarded with a slurpy kiss across the side of her face.

"Better than Sugar at least." John gave her a mischievous grin.

Erin laughed. "That wouldn't be hard." Wait till Cassie heard about Veronica and Sugar.

The Jeep turned at the familiar Dove Creek Kennels sign and rolled past the holly bushes. "Looks like your grandma has company," John remarked.

Erin's eyes widened. It was an SUV. Her parents' SUV! A figure waved from the porch.

"Mom!" Erin yelled. She threw open the door and raced up the stairs. Excited by the sudden movement, Blue jumped down from the Jeep. "You're early," Erin shouted. And Blue barked in agreement.

—————————— • ⬭

"So when your dad lined up a few job interviews, I got someone to take my classes for a few days and we decided to come early," Erin's mom explained. "That way we can spend some extra time together and be well rested for the show." She reached out to touch Erin's hair for a second time. "I just love that color on you."

Erin grinned. "Thanks, Mom." Her mother hadn't said a word about her legs and she hadn't noticed that her warts were practically invisible, but she had noticed her hair as soon as Erin had jumped from the Jeep. Mom's mouth had fallen open. She had stretched out her hand and touched it like she'd never seen Erin's hair before. And her father had made a crack about Erin being too young to mess with stuff like that. But then Grandma had rushed outside and come to her rescue by saying how nice it was that Erin had picked such a pretty color instead of the blues and greens some young people were choosing. Dad shut his mouth; Mom smiled and agreed. And that had been that.

Erin scooped up the last piece of her strawberry cheesecake, her most favorite-in-the-whole-wide-world dessert that her mother had brought special delivery from the North Shore Bakery. "Youftshppes."

"Finish your mouthful, bug-face." Erin could tell her father wasn't really angry; in fact, he looked happier and more relaxed than Erin had seen him in a long time.

"You have to see the puppies!" She licked the strawberry glaze from her fork as she glanced from her father to her mother. "You haven't seen them yet, have you?"

"We asked but Grandma said we had to wait for you."

"Something about you assisting in the delivery room." Her father's eyes twinkled above his coffee cup.

"You should have seen it," Erin said as she led her parents down the hall. "It was great!"

Duchess greeted them with a thump of her tail, and the movement woke Arnie and Gumby. Erin reached for Gumby and cradled him against her chest. "See?" She said, holding out his foot. "I put the nail polish on his toe."

Arnie began to whimper and Mom laughed. "Come here," Erin said, lifting the stocky yellow Lab from the crate.

Erin pointed to the corner where several of the puppies were curled up together. "That's Mercedes, she's the prettiest. And Honey, she's the nicest. And Fred is the loudest."

"That must be Twister." Dad gestured to the black puppy eyeing them from the other side of the crate.

Nodding, she put Gumby down and reached for him. "He has a problem with his leg."

"Grandma told us."

Erin held Twister against her cheek. The puppy didn't squirm like the rest of the litter; he barely moved in her hand. His fur was soft, like the rabbit's foot charm she kept in her desk at school. "I want to take him home!"

Erin's parents were both silent.

"I've been working with him every single day. I can make him walk, I know I can. I'll work with him twice a day even," she promised. "You said when I showed some responsibility I could have a pet. I've been helping Grandma a lot and working with John and Blue every day and I'm going to try and get on as a volunteer at the SPCA this fall. A volunteer," she stressed again. "Which is pretty responsible since everybody knows kids need money but I don't care about that because all I want to do is work with dogs!" She was out of breath.

Her parents glanced at each other and then back at Erin. Her mother's mouth was set in what Erin called her "crumble smile"—the smile she used when she was trying not to cry. Her father fiddled with his earlobe. Dad only fiddled with his earlobe when he was uncomfortable.

Erin stroked Twister and whispered in his ear. This morning when she'd done that, he had twitched and licked at her fingers. This afternoon he did nothing. He was soft and limp in her hand. "Twister will be fine," she told her parents. "He just needs extra love and attention, that's all." She stroked his tiny head.

"He's badly injured," Mom said softly. "We can't take care of him."

"I can. You don't have to do anything!"

"Let me have a look," her father said gruffly. He held out his hand.

She handed Twister to her father. "Careful," she cautioned as her father held Twister high in the air and studied him.

"He has a nice face."

"Steve," Mom warned.

Erin's heart jumped. The sweet taste of hope tingled in her mouth. Dad liked him. She could tell. "He's a beauty, Dad! And he'd make a great pet. Just look how quiet and laid-back he is. He wouldn't be a jumper or a chewer. Not this one."

Her father stroked Twister's head for a minute before putting him back into the corner of the crate. "It's up to Grandma, bug-face. She may not be letting him go home with anyone." He straightened and reached for Erin. "Besides, first things first." He gave her shoulders a squeeze. "I understand there's a dog show to win!"

Chapter Fifteen

"SENIOR NOVICE." Would all those participating in Senior Novice, Junior Division, please bring themselves and their dogs to the starting position? Thank you very much."

"That's you!" Cassie gave her a hug.

Erin nodded and licked her lips. Her mouth was dry and toasty, filled with a stale, leftover popcorn taste. The taste of nervousness.

The wind caught a corner of her hair. She smoothed it back into place. A light breeze swept through the crowd at the Comox Valley Exhibition Grounds, cooling the hot midday sun, gently lifting the bottoms of skirts and tugging playfully at sun hats.

John led Erin and Cassie past clusters of dogs and owners to the show ring and the nearby seats. Blue strolled happily beside them.

"You look great," Cassie whispered in her ear. "The perfect reinvention worked!"

Erin grinned. It had been worth it. Every single glob of that smelly henna, every painful tweeze of her eyebrows, that horrible cream and self-tanner that had burned her legs. She had reinvented herself in time for the Comox Valley Dog Show. "Thanks, Cass," she whispered back.

"It's time." John came to a stop outside the ring.

Erin's heart pounded so hard she was sure if she looked down her top would be moving in time to the beat. She smoothed the pink skirt and reached for Blue's leash.

"You can do this," John reminded her again as he fastened the number card around the top of her arm. "You're well prepared and so is Blue."

A monarch butterfly circled in the sunlight a few feet away and Blue lunged for it. Erin pulled on his leash. "Behave, Blue!" she ordered.

"Good luck." John gave her arm one last pat and then he was gone. Cassie gave her the thumbs-up sign and followed him to their seats.

With a firm hold on Blue, she headed for the ring. *Thrump, thrump, thrump*. She wondered if anyone had ever died from a pounding heart before. Her mother and father waved from their seats as she went by. Grandma gave her a grin and blew her a kiss. Erin gave them all a weak smile.

All of a sudden this dog show seemed like a really dumb idea!

Even with the perfect reinvention.

It felt as if she were walking through a field of mashed potatoes as she headed for her starting position. What if she tripped over her feet like she sometimes did?

Or worse, tripped over Blue?

Squished him flat like a pancake!

Her skirt would fly up in the air.

Everyone would know Erin Morris was the same old klutz she had always been.

So much for perfection.

"Number please?" It was the same man who had surveyed the field just a few days earlier.

"Forty-four," she mumbled.

The man frowned. "Pardon?"

"Forty-four!"

"Hmm." The man scanned down his clipboard. "Right; there you are. Erin Morris." He made a check beside her name. "You're beside McClanahan." He gestured toward the middle of the line. "The girl wearing turquoise, with the brown Pomeranian."

Great! Just her luck there were no midsized dogs between the Pomeranian and Blue. She was going to be stuck beside Sugar for the entire show.

"*Eii, eii, eii.*"

Erin swallowed a nervous giggle. Then again, the other dog was bound to make Blue look good! "Hello." She took her spot behind Veronica. "Isn't it nice that our dogs will be beside each other?" She gave the girl an innocent smile.

Sugar began to do contortions again. "*Eii, eii, eii,*" she yelped, her buggy eyes firmly fastened on Blue.

"Not really," Veronica said rudely. She stuck her warthog nose in the air. "My dog doesn't like your dog."

So much for friendliness. "We can't all have good taste," Erin snapped.

"*Eii, eii, eii.*" Sugar was getting louder. People were staring. Erin watched as Veronica clamped a large, square hand over the Pomeranian's mouth. "Shut up, Sugar," Veronica hissed.

The line filled up quickly. Behind Erin was a tall, thin boy with a beautiful Boxer named Oscar. The boy gave Erin a shy smile. Oscar and Blue wagged their tails at each other but seemed perfectly content to stand quietly and wait for the judging to begin.

Not Sugar. Sugar yelped every time a new dog ventured within twenty yards of her territory. Veronica McClanahan was getting more and more frustrated. She ought to feel sorry for her, Erin thought. But why feel sorry for someone who was so mean?

The judge walked into the ring. Erin straightened her shoulders and tightened her hold on Blue's leash.

"Ladies and gentlemen, we are about to begin."

Erin's heart sped up. "Steady, Blue." She exchanged glances with Oscar's owner, who whispered, "Good luck." She smiled and nodded her thanks back. Sugar started howling.

"Take your animals into the ring, please," the judge instructed. "And take up your positions."

Erin and Blue were right in the middle of the pack. She waited almost a minute for the line to begin moving. Once it did, she let Veronica and Sugar get a good start. The last thing she wanted was Blue spooked because of that dog's yipping.

Sugar wasn't howling at Blue. She was howling at the Great Dane in front of her. Making so much noise, in fact, that Veronica was forced to pull her along.

It was like walking behind a pull toy.

As she passed the judge, Erin pretended she was perfectly used to walking behind pull toys. She flashed the man a confident smile.

"Tail up," she urged Blue. Blue's tail went higher.

"Steady on," she coached. Blue's pacing was smooth; his gait excellent.

"Good work, Blue." Erin heaped praise all over the dog once they were still and he was in the correct position. She reached into her skirt pocket for a dog biscuit and he crunched it enthusiastically.

"*Eii, eii, eii.*" Sugar didn't like the sound of Blue's crunching. "*Eii, eii, eii.*"

"Would you please refrain from feeding your animal?" Veronica McClanahan sniffed. "Sugar doesn't like it."

"*Eii, eii, eii.*" By the sound of it, Sugar didn't like much.

"Would number eleven please control her animal?" the judge asked loudly. All eyes turned to Erin's end of the field.

Number eleven. Veronica McClanahan. Erin watched the girl's hand clamp itself around Sugar's face. This time Erin did feel sorry. For the dog. Sugar just wasn't show material.

"Bait and stack your dogs, please," the judge said next.

Stacking was simply a matter of putting your dog in the proper standing position. Erin had practiced it on Blue hundreds of times. Now she corrected Blue's front foot, lifted his chin and stretched his tail into place. She made herself go slow and steady. She could feel the judge watching her. So far, so good.

Veronica, on the other hand, was struggling with Sugar, who had to be stacked on a table. The little dog was skidding and sliding, running from one hand to the other as if they were playing a game. How embarrassing! Erin fought back a smile and looked away.

"Perhaps we'll have the animals walk a pattern in a group first so they have a chance to work off some steam." The judge's eyes swept over the dogs, lingering a little too long on poor old Sugar. "The triangle pattern, please."

Blue's favorite pattern and hers, too, Erin thought. The line began to move. Oscar and his owner started to walk. Erin counted off five seconds before she issued the command to Blue. The Retriever moved out in a straight line. His head was up and his tail was proudly displayed. He took the first turn perfectly. And the second. Erin slowed as she passed the judge, just as John had instructed.

"Perfect! Good boy." Erin scratched him vigorously behind the ears. She glanced over to the spectators and caught a glimpse of Cassie, wildly waving her arms in encouragement. Her grandmother was grinning broadly, and John was giving her the thumbs-up signal. Erin smiled. She and Blue had to be getting a good score!

"Assume your positions, please. Individual judging is about to begin."

The line stretched out, with dogs and owners spaced neatly apart. The judge headed for the middle of the line—straight for Veronica McClanahan and Sugar. Erin looked at Blue and held her finger to her lips. "Quiet, Blue," she murmured as she continued to bait and stack him.

"And your dog's name is?" The judge gave Veronica a friendly smile.

Sugar jumped off the table. "*Eii, eii, eii, eii.*" The Pomeranian lunged for the man's feet.

Erin tried hard not to giggle. Blue shuffled his feet; Erin quickly moved him back into position.

"Sugar." Veronica lifted Sugar up and held her tight. "Er, Sugar McClanahan the Third. And normally she's pretty quiet. I'm not sure what's up today."

Erin looked at Oscar's owner and rolled her eyes. He raised his eyebrows and grinned back.

"I see. Yes." The judge offered Veronica a sympathetic smile. "And what is her breed?"

"Pomeranian," Veronica said, but before she could continue, Sugar took over.

"*Eii, eii, eii, eii, eii.*"

The girl slapped her hand over Sugar's nose and raised her voice. "She's spooked by some of these other bigger dogs." She gave Blue a dirty look before she turned back to the judge. "She took all firsts in her puppy class last summer."

Erin smirked. Puppy class for noise and rudeness, probably.

"That's fine, miss." The judge was getting impatient. "Stack her again, please."

Veronica set Sugar into position on the table. "Stay," she ordered in a wavery voice. But the dog yapped twice and then jumped up and bit Veronica's nose before squatting and peeing on the table.

The judge winced and looked away. "I'll come back to you," he promised, moving away.

He stopped in front of Erin and Blue. Blue's tail wagged. The judge smiled and turned to Erin. "Dog's name, please?" he asked.

"Mr. Lavender Blue," she answered swiftly. "From Dove Creek Kennels in Courtenay." She knelt beside Blue. Her hand held the leash steady at his neck, and she kept her other hand behind his tail. Blue looked great! His front and hindquarters were perfectly placed, just like John had taught her. His head was forward; he held his position patiently.

The judge nodded approvingly, circled Blue and

made a few comments in his book. "Very nice." He patted Blue on the head and smiled. "I have a few questions for your handler now. You can relax for a few minutes."

Blue wagged his tail again. Erin looked over, saw John grinning and forced herself to breathe.

"What group does Blue belong to?" the judge asked.

"The sporting group," Erin answered promptly, "which consists of Pointers and Setters, Retrievers and Spaniels."

"And what are the main characteristics of your dog?"

Erin recited from memory.

"What is the difference between yellow and black Flat-Coated Retrievers?" he asked.

Erin grinned. It was a trick question and she was prepared for it. "There are no yellow Flat-Coated Retrievers," she replied swiftly. "Only black and liver-colored ones. And color doesn't make a difference to the breed."

The judge flashed a smile. After a few more questions about breed history, temperament, and health problems, he said, "Let's examine Blue, shall we?"

Erin bent down and the judge continued to question her. "Show me his hip, please."

Erin pointed.

"His tail?"

Too easy. Erin pointed again.

"How about his stifle?"

Erin hesitated. The stifle was on the leg somewhere. She ran her hand up from Blue's foot and when she reached his hock, she remembered. "There," she said, pointing to Blue's knee.

"Good." The judge nodded. "And where is his breastbone?"

His breastbone. Erin frowned. Dogs didn't have breastbones. Or did they? She stared at Blue's chest. What if she was wrong? "I don't—" She stopped. She might be wrong. But she had to take that chance. "Dogs don't have breastbones," she said.

"Well done!" the judge said with a satisfied look on his face. He turned his attention back to Blue. "Would you show me his bite, please?"

Erin froze. The mouth exam hadn't been a sure thing. John had said some judges did it and some didn't. Blue hated having his mouth touched. And no one could get him to open it if he didn't want to—no one, not even John. Brushing his teeth every day had been torture.

She felt eyes on her: dogs' eyes, people's eyes, the judge's eyes. They were waiting for her for her to issue the command. But Erin was afraid to. Blue might not obey. Then the winning ribbon, the ribbon she and Blue had worked so hard for, wouldn't go to him at all. It would go to some other dog.

"Well," the judge said brightly. "Come on."

"I—" Erin opened her mouth to explain but stopped herself. John had told her over and over again that no matter what Blue did, she should never make excuses for him. Like Veronica had done for Sugar.

"Okay." Taking a deep breath, Erin put one hand on top of Blue's head and the other under his chin. The judge knelt down to take a close look.

Blue would not open his mouth.

Come on, Blue, Erin urged silently. *We've come this far. Don't blow it now!* She worked his mouth with her hands.

Blue's mouth still wouldn't budge.

Oscar's owner gave her a sympathetic look. Erin stared hard at Blue, willing him to open his mouth. The dog stared stubbornly back.

The judge glanced up at Erin. "Do you say something special to him?"

"Not really." Erin squeezed the dog's chin. "Open, Blue," she said sternly.

Blue clenched his teeth.

Desperation powered Erin's hands. She wedged

her fingers into Blue's mouth. "Open!" She pried his jaw apart.

Blue opened his mouth.

The judge nodded vigorously. "Very good." He leaned over and gave his teeth a leisurely examination.

Hurry up, hurry up! Erin chanted under her breath. *Before he snaps his jaw shut again.*

Finally the judge straightened. "Thank you," he said. "Walk Mr. Lavender Blue in an L pattern, please."

Off they went. It wasn't Blue's best walk. He was tired. Erin was still shaking from the mouth examination. Blue went too fast in a few spots and Erin stumbled over a rock in front of the spectators.

She could squish him flat like a pancake.

Her skirt could fly into the air.

And everyone would know she was the same old klutz.

"Thank you." The judge nodded when she returned.

She'd blown it. For sure! Erin watched the judge move on to Oscar and his owner. She paid little attention as the owners went through the routine of baiting, stacking, and answering questions. She was reviewing Blue's performance. Her own performance. Maybe she hadn't blown it. Maybe she still had a chance.

She worried over every single little detail.

She wondered where she would place.

"Please stand by," the announcer said. "The winners will be revealed momentarily."

A thin line of sweat trickled between her shoulder blades to the small of her back. Her forehead was damp, her hands clammy. Blue was getting restless. She baited and stacked him again. He looked up at her with big, trusting eyes. *Now what?* he seemed to be saying. "Shhh," she whispered. Soon it would be over. Soon she would know.

"Before making my final decision, I'd like to ask the handlers to take their dogs around the ring once more," the judge announced.

Erin's heart thumped wildly. Judges only did that when they were having trouble making a decision. Handlers and dogs began to move. A sudden hush fell over the crowd. Everyone seemed to know how close the decision was. Even Sugar was strangely quiet and well behaved. The walk around the ring seemed to take forever. Erin felt like she was walking through mashed potatoes all over again. Finally it was over. Dogs and owners returned to their standing positions.

The judge looked at each couple in turn. Handler and dog. Handler and dog. Erin licked her lips nervously. That last walk had been perfect, but the one before hadn't. Maybe she and Blue would come in second. It was probably about as close to perfect as she was going to get.

"I am pleased to—" A wild bout of coughing overcame the man and he stopped.

Not now! Blue stirred restlessly and Erin jerked on his leash. "Sit still," she whispered.

"Excuse me." He accepted a glass of water and took a long drink. "That's better." The judge gave one last cough and smiled at the crowd. "As I was about to say, I am pleased to announce my decision."

The judge walked across the ring toward her. Erin felt light-headed, dizzy. He stood in front of her and pointed. "First," he pronounced loudly. He moved down the line, pointing out second and third in quick succession.

At first Erin wasn't sure she'd heard right.

Everyone clapped, which made Sugar start her *eii, eii* noises again, and then Blue barked, which made everyone laugh. It was all very confusing, until Erin saw Veronica glare at her and Oscar's owner smile shyly and motion her forward.

She and Blue had won!

Erin was floating. She wasn't walking through mashed potatoes anymore. She was floating through clouds. Grinning harder than she'd ever grinned in her life. Grinning so hard she was sure her face was going to crack.

"Congratulations." The judge moved the winning dogs and their handlers into place and then quickly handed out ribbons—a large, blue first place ribbon for her and Blue. Just as she was being ushered away for a picture, Erin looked up and saw Cassie waving wildly...her parents clapping and grinning...John looking happy and proud...and her grandmother jumping up and down with excitement.

She had won. She and Blue had really won.

And then Erin tasted it! The taste of perfection. It filled her mouth and bubbled down her throat. It was better than anything she had ever tasted before. Better than the best cheesecake from the North Shore Bakery. Better than her favorite ice cream float. Better than blueberries fresh from the bush.

Perfection was something Erin Morris had never tasted before. And it was a taste she would never forget.

Blue was perfect. She was perfect. There was another dog show in Campbell River next week. That would be perfect, too. Because Blue would win again. She knew it.

She had tasted perfection. And she wanted to taste it again.

Chapter Sixteen

"**I** KNEW YOU COULD DO IT!" Grandma beamed from the easy chair in the corner of the living room. "There wasn't a doubt in my mind that you and Blue would win." She reached down and gave Blue's head a scratch. "He's such a champ, this one." Blue was tired of being the center of attention. He yawned and stretched out for a well-earned nap.

John scraped up the last of the crumbs from the chocolate cake he'd bought to celebrate. "I was worried when I saw the judge wanted to do a mouth exam." He licked his fork and put his plate on the coffee table.

"Me, too!" Erin said. "Especially when Blue wouldn't open his mouth right away." She had just finished talking on the phone with Rachel and was sprawled out on the floor beside Blue. "And then he walked too fast during the L pattern and I stumbled on that rock." She shook her head in wonder. "I didn't think we'd win after that."

"You did a fabulous job, darlin'. You helped me out and showed a great deal of responsibility at the same time." Grandma put her coffee down on the nearby table. "Blue's come a long way in the weeks you've worked with him. This win has given him valuable points. If he keeps on like this, he'll be earning more ribbons than I have space for." She laughed at her own joke.

"Your dad and I are very proud of you," Mom said. "And not just because you and Blue won, either."

"That's right, bug-face." Her father had taken up his familiar after-dinner pose, reclining in the corner of the couch, one arm stretched out beside him. "You worked hard this summer and it shows."

She brought her knees under her chest, folded her arms around them, and rocked back and forth. "So can I have a dog then? Pleeeease?" She glanced from her father to her mother. "Let me have Twister! I can take care of him. I can make him walk. I know I can. Pleeeease?"

"I'm not sure you'll have time for a dog," Dad said. "You're going to be pretty busy come September."

Erin rolled her eyes. "I can handle grade eight, Dad. You just wait and see." She had spent the last half hour on the phone filling Rachel in on all the changes—her plum perfect hair, her tanned legs, and her wart-free left hand. Not to mention the dog show win!

"Er, that's not quite what I meant." Dad cleared his throat. "I didn't want to tell you before the show in case you got distracted, but I heard back from the SPCA. They've got a volunteer spot for you this September, if you still want it."

"Want it?" Erin shrieked. "Of course I want it!" First the win, now this. Everything was working out perfectly! "I'll be able to volunteer at the SPCA and handle grade eight and look after Twister. Pleeeease?" she begged again.

Her mother and father looked at each other before looking at Grandma.

Erin's heart skittered into her throat. They were thinking about it. "I'll take such good care of him. I'll teach him to walk. I'll groom him and work with him. I'll even train him, just like John taught me. Maybe next year we can do three or four shows together!" She stopped rocking and leaned close to her grandmother. "Please, Grandma? I promise you I'll take perfect care of Twister. *Extra* perfect care."

Grandma Morris looked at Erin for a long time without saying anything. "I'm afraid that's not possible, darlin'," she finally said.

"What do you mean, not possible?"

There was a look in her grandmother's eyes that Erin had never seen before. "Dr. Maartens came and took Twister away," she said softly. "While we were at the show."

At first Erin misunderstood. "But he'll be back, right? After the doctor examines him again?"

Grandma shook her head. "Erin, Twister was failing badly. He hadn't been eating. His heart was giving out." Grandma's eyes were overly bright, like she was about to cry. "He'd never walk. It just wasn't possible. We put him down, darlin'. It was the best thing for him."

For a minute, Erin felt paralyzed. Then fear twisted her stomach, rolled through her like a runaway train. "How could you?" She stared at her grandmother. "He was a beautiful, innocent puppy. So gentle and quiet." She forced the words out around the lump in her throat. "He would have made a perfect pet. Just perfect."

"You don't understand, darlin'—," Grandma tried to explain.

"You're right," Erin's voice began to climb. "I *don't* understand. That was a mean, awful thing to do."

"Erin." Her father's voice issued a warning.

"There will be other dogs, Erin," Mom said.

"Your grandmother did what she had to do," John added. "As cruel as it sounds, some animals aren't meant to live. Putting them to sleep is the kindest thing to do."

The lump in Erin's throat grew bigger. Tears gathered behind her eyes. "It's wrong!"

Blue stood up and whined.

Erin stared at them all: her grandmother and John, her mother and father. They were so big. So mean! And Twister was so little! So helpless. "I'm going to Cassie's!" She jumped up and bolted for the back door. Cassie would understand. She always did.

"Wait until you're calm," Grandma urged.

"Wait at least five—"

The rest of her mother's words were lost in the slamming of the door. "Come on, Blue!" Erin grabbed her bike from the shed. "We're going for a ride."

She was out the gate and down the road before she realized she had forgotten her helmet. And forgotten Blue's harness. The springer bounced gently, its unattached end slapping softly against the road.

"Too bad," she muttered under her breath as she pumped the pedals on the bike. She wasn't going back. Not now. Not later, either. She'd stay overnight at Cassie's place. She'd stay there for the rest of the summer if she could.

Blue was as happy as Erin was sad. He raced ahead of Erin, jumping at a monarch butterfly, barking at a sparrow. He loved running beside the bike. And tonight he loved his freedom.

The wind whipped her hair into a stinging frenzy. Impatiently she pushed it away. Faster, faster, faster, she pedaled. Poor Twister. Poor, poor Twister. Gone forever!

There was a movement in the bushes across the road. She slowed for the corner and glanced left. There was a flash of beige, a tip of white.

A deer!

Blue saw it, too.

"Wait, Blue," she warned. She could hear a car up ahead.

"*Woof!*" The dog charged across the road to chase the deer.

Brakes screeched.

"Blue!"

There was a thud of flesh hitting metal.

For a minute there was stillness. And then the air was filled with the piercing and inhuman sound of an animal howling in desperate and confused agony.

Chapter Seventeen

"**N**OOOOOOOOOOOOOO!" Erin's bike went one way; she went the other. She stared down at the still, dark ball curled up against the base of a tire. He should be barking...chasing butterflies...running in circles around her bike. "Blue! Get up, Blue! Get up!" If only she'd put him on the stringer. If only he hadn't run into the road after the deer.

Helpless, Blue looked up at her. His dark eyes were huge and shiny. His howls had turned to soft whimpers. From very far away came the sound of a car door slamming—the sound of footsteps approaching.

All Erin could see or hear or think about was Blue. She threw herself on the ground beside him. "Blue. Oh, Blue." She buried her face in his fur of his neck. "Blue. Mr. Lavender Blue. My champion. My love. I'm sorry. I'm so sorry," she sobbed. "I should have remembered the harness and put you on the springer. It's all my fault. I'm sorry, Blue. I'm so, so sorry."

Blue whimpered again. Something was staining the ground underneath him. Blood! All of a sudden her stomach felt queasy; she tasted the chocolate cake she'd had for dessert.

"We have to call for help," a shaky voice said.

Erin brushed the tears from her eyes and looked up. Sheila Jones, her face round and frightened, stared down at her. Actually she was staring at Blue. "I—I...I didn't see him. I wasn't going fast. I'm sure I wasn't. I was thinking about the lovely dog I'm picking up next week from your grandmother. The one you call Arnie." Mrs. Jones was babbling. In her hand was a cell phone.

A phone! Erin reached out to grab it but Mrs. Jones was gesturing so wildly Erin couldn't get it. And the woman was still talking. "We have to call for help," she said again, her shocked eyes remaining on Blue. "He just ran right out in front of me. I felt the bump the same time I saw him. He was running very fast. Where is his leash?" Mrs. Jones seemed to remember Erin was there. She looked up. Her face was the same gray as the gravel on the road. "Did it come off?" She glanced around. "Where is it?"

She gulped. "I—"

Blue whimpered. Erin turned back to Blue. She laid a hand on the dog's neck. She didn't want to be away from him for a minute. "Phone 911," she cried over her shoulder. "The police. Or...or somebody."

Sheila Jones seemed incapable of speaking. "I...I..."

Blue let out a howl.

Erin's stomach lurched. The dog needed help now. She'd have to do it herself!

She snatched the phone from her grandmother's friend. Her fingers were shaking. It took her three tries just to punch out 911. Her voice quavered as she spoke. "Just before the Walker flower farm," she told the operator. "On Dove Creek Road. Hurry!" she urged.

"There, Blue." She leaned over and rubbed her face against Blue's ear. Her tears made his black fur gleam in the dusky evening light. "The operator said she'd call the SPCA. They'll send a truck soon. I promise!" The blood stain was growing. Erin wouldn't look. Of course, there was blood, she told herself as she took a deep breath. There was a cut for sure. Maybe even a broken leg. But help was coming. Blue would be fine.

Everything would be fine!

"They're coming," she reassured Mrs. Jones, who was leaning against the car, holding her hand over her mouth and looking like she was going to be sick. For a minute Erin almost felt sorry for her.

The woman's head bobbed up and down vigorously. "Good," she said. "I'm so sorry…" She stopped and pressed her trembling lips together. Her eyes remained fixed on Erin. She knew she was trying not to look at Blue. "Your grandmother is my—" Sheila Jones stopped again. "I'm so sorry," she repeated.

Her grandmother! She had to call her grandmother. Erin's fingers were steady now as she punched out the familiar number. Dogs got hit by cars all the time. Blue would be fine. Just fine! At the sound of her grandmother's "hello," Erin's courage flew. She began to sob. What if…what if Blue wasn't fine? It would be all her fault.

"G—G…rrranndma."

"What is it?" Grandma's voice was sharp with alarm. "What's wrong?"

"I'm—I'm—I'm sorry."

"What is it?" Grandma repeated. "What's happened?"

Erin swallowed her tears. "There's been an accident."

"Are you all right? Where are you? Are you hurt? Just slow down, darlin'. Speak slowly."

"I'm…I'm on the road to Cassie's. There was a deer. A car. Mrs. Jones. It's Blue." The tears started again. "He's hurt, Grandma. There's blood." Erin glanced down. "A...a lot of blood. I'm so scared."

"We'll be right there, darlin'. Right there!"

And they were. It seemed like Erin had just handed the phone back when John's Jeep came rushing up the road. Her mother flew to her side, while John, Grandma and her father ran to Blue. Sheila Jones hovered between the two groups, wringing her hands and saying over and over again, "He just ran right out in front of me. I felt the bump the same time I saw him."

"Are you okay, sweetheart?" Mom cupped Erin's face with her hands before pulling back to give her arms and legs a quick once-over. "Did you get hit, too? Are you all right?"

She nodded. "I'm fine. But Blue—" She wiped her eyes with the back of her hand. "Blue's hurt." John and Grandma were huddled around the dog; Erin couldn't see what they were doing.

"I know," her mother said softly. "We called for help but it sounds like you beat us to it. Good girl," she added.

She wasn't a good girl at all! She was awful. She'd forgotten to put Blue on the springer. She didn't deserve to have a dog of her own. Why hadn't she taken more care? Why hadn't she gone back for the harness? Why hadn't Mrs. Jones stayed home and watched TV tonight? She glared at the woman, who was now talking to Dad in a quick, scared voice. "Came running out of nowhere," Erin heard her say.

"She was going too fast," she whispered to her mother in a tight, hard voice. "Way too fast!"

"Don't worry about that right now, Erin," her mother replied. "Let's deal with Blue first."

"What if...what if..." Her voice cracked. "What if Blue dies?"

Mom's arms went around Erin. "Look," she urged. "See that?"

Erin looked. Coming around the corner was an SPCA truck with the words Animal Hospital printed across the bottom.

"Help's here. They're going to do everything they can to make sure Blue makes it. Everything!" her mother promised fiercely.

———— •◯ ————

Erin sat hunched in the corner of the couch, staring at the hands on her grandmother's old mantel clock: 10:30. Her grandmother had promised to phone as soon as Dr. Maartens looked at Blue. That had been almost two hours ago.

Dad looked up from his crossword puzzle. "You should get to bed, bug-face."

"You said I could wait till Grandma called." Erin pulled her knees under her chin and rocked slowly back and forth. How could a day that had started out perfectly turn out so perfectly awful? First, Twister.

Now Blue.

Twister had been horrible. Awful.

But what had happened to Blue was worse. Erin remembered the words John had used to describe Blue in the car just a few days ago. Full of spit and vinegar. Then she thought of Blue lying in a heap on the side of the road. Whimpering. Staring up at her with those big, shiny eyes. His spit and vinegar was gone.

And it was all her fault. Sheila Jones insisted she hadn't been speeding. She had been driving below the speed limit. She always did.

Erin believed her.

Blue's accident was all her fault. There was no one else to blame.

If only she had remembered the harness. If only Blue hadn't chased after that deer. If only…if only.

"Here's your hot chocolate." Mom laid a tray on the coffee table and glanced at the clock herself. "I think eleven o'clock is late enough." She handed Erin a mug. "How about it?"

Erin shook her head. "You said I could wait till

they called. And they promised they'd call as soon as they had news."

Please, God, let Blue be okay, Erin begged silently. *I'll never ask for anything else as long as I live. Please, God, don't let Blue die. Let him be full of spit and vinegar again.*

"Drink up," her mother urged.

Erin tapped a marshmallow and watched it slowly dissolve into the brown liquid. Everything had been so perfect—the perfect reinvention...the perfect dog show...the perfect Mr. Lavender Blue. But not now. Not anymore.

A stream of light shot through the open window. Headlights. They were back! Erin jumped up so fast that her hot chocolate slopped over the side of the cup.

"Careful!" Mom warned as she took the cup from Erin.

Dad put down his crossword puzzle book and stood. One Jeep door slammed...and then the other.

Erin waited. For a second she almost expected Blue to come running ahead as he always did. But he didn't. Not tonight.

"Come on, bug-face." Her father dropped his arm casually on Erin's shoulder and propelled her in the direction of the door. "Let's go see how he is."

Grandma and John leaned against the side of the Jeep, talking quietly. The light from the living room dusted their faces in a pale glow, but it wasn't bright enough to tell Erin how they were feeling.

They were quiet as Erin and her parents approached.

How is he? Erin wanted to scream. But she was silent; embarrassed that she had caused this trouble...this pain.

"How is he?" Erin's father spoke for her.

"He lost a lot of blood." John sounded tired.

Erin swallowed. *Please, God,* she begged again. *Please, God.* "Is he...is he...?"

"He's alive," Grandma whispered softly in the darkness. "But he's in pretty bad shape. Let's go inside." She moved toward the stairs. "I need to sit down."

"I just made hot chocolate," Mom said after Grandma sank slowly into a kitchen chair. "How about some?"

John shook his head as he took the chair beside Grandma. "No thanks."

"Sounds good," Grandma said wearily. "I'm feeling a touch cold tonight."

Erin had never seen her grandmother look so pale or so worn out. The morning after the puppies were born she had looked tired. Tonight her brown eyes were shadowed and her face was haggard. She looked exhausted.

Don't cry. Don't cry! Erin fought back the tears that were gathering again. "I'm so sorry," she whispered to her grandmother as she stood hesitantly in the doorway. "It's all my fault and I'm so, so sorry."

Grandma nodded. She opened her mouth to speak and then shut it. Her eyes stayed on the mug of chocolate Erin's mother placed in front of her.

Say something, Erin wanted to scream. *Anything!*

John spoke instead. "Accidents happen," he said gently. "We all know that." He took Grandma's hand.

"How is... Will Blue...will he be all right?" Erin asked.

Her grandmother finally raised her eyes to look at Erin. "The operation's over. We'll just have to wait and see how Blue does through the night." Grandma's voice was strained.

Erin's heart began to pound. "Operation?"

Grandma nodded. "They amputated, m'darlin'."

Erin went cold with shock. "Amputated?" She stared at her grandmother. "What do you mean...amputated?" The word was repulsive and frightening.

Grandma looked at John. John looked at Erin. "Blue lost one of his front legs," he explained gently.

"No!" She felt her face crumble. The thought of amputation hadn't occurred to her.

"The vet had a choice," John said. "It was either that or let him bleed to death. We all wanted to save him."

The tears Erin had been holding back began to fall. She leaned against the wall for support. "No leg?" She shook her head in disbelief. "But he won't be able to walk or run or...or—" A sob stopped her. Blue wouldn't be going to the Campbell River Dog Show. Or any other dog show. Ever again.

He wasn't a champion anymore.

He wasn't perfect.

All because she had forgotten to use the springer.

Her mother reached for Erin's hand and gave it a squeeze.

She peered out through her tears. "That's—that's—that's horrible." *Majorly* horrible, as Cassie would say. And it was all her fault. Disgust flooded her.

"It's not good," Grandma agreed. "But if he survives the next few days and makes it through physical therapy, he'll be all right. A little the worse for the experience, but he should learn to walk again."

"But he'll have no quality of life," Erin said thickly. How could she have forgotten the harness? How *could* she have done it?

"He won't be a show dog anymore," John added. "But he'll still make a fine and loving pet."

Erin stared at him. Blue. Full of spit and vinegar. The dog that couldn't wait to get up in the morning to chase birds or bring sticks. The dog that loved to chase butterflies and run beside her bike. The dog that won this year's junior showmanship class.

The perfect Mr. Lavender Blue was perfect no more. All because she had been angry and upset and in too much of a hurry to get to Cassie's house. Erin couldn't choke back her sobs anymore. Angry and ashamed, she ran from the kitchen to the safety of her room.

Chapter Eighteen

THE BACK OF THE APPLE TREE dug uncomfortably into her spine. Erin yawned and shifted her position slightly. She was tired; she hadn't slept well since the accident four days ago. Blue had come through that first night and then the next. According to Dr. Maartens, he was going to be fine.

He wasn't fine. And neither was she. She'd never be fine again.

The late afternoon sun hung lower in the sky these days. The apples were starting to fall. Summer was almost over. In a few days, she would be going home.

Restlessly she tapped at a windfall apple with her toe. Once upon a time, Blue would have been there to chase it. Now the slightly lopsided piece of fruit rolled forward slightly and stopped. She could see a large black wormhole near the stem.

A worm. That's what she was. A worm.

Even if she didn't say a thing about the accident to Rachel, even if no one in school knew about Blue, she'd still be a worm. A stupid worm. And stupid worms didn't deserve to work at the SPCA.

She had made a mistake and it had cost Blue his leg. It had almost cost him his life.

A door slammed. Erin looked up. Grandma headed slowly from the kennel run to the house, the feed bowl tucked carefully under her arm. Was it her imagination, Erin wondered, or did her grandmother look older all of a sudden? Sadder maybe?

Grandma glanced to the right, saw Erin, and changed direction. "It'll be dinnertime soon," she said when she reached the tree. "Your mother's pot roast smells good."

Erin nodded. When her father left to start his new job, her mother announced she was staying at the farm with Erin. The person she'd found to fill in for three days at camp had agreed to stay on and teach the final week. Mom said she deserved a little extra holiday time. Erin knew she had stayed behind because of Blue.

Slowly Grandma lowered herself to the ground. "Can I share your spot?" she asked.

Erin nodded a second time.

Her grandmother leaned back. "I want to tell you a story." She reached for her hand.

"Okay."

"Once upon a time there was a girl, there was a dog, and there was a grandmother. The girl wanted to take her bike and the dog to the river. She asked her grandmother for permission."

Erin swallowed the lump in her throat. Her grandmother squeezed her hand and continued. "The grandmother knew all about leashes and harnesses and springers, but the grandmother also knew about freedom. And so she said yes."

Erin's eyes filled with tears.

"There was an accident," Grandma continued gravely. "And the dog was hurt. Badly hurt. The girl felt terrible. So did the grandmother. The accident wouldn't have happened if a mistake hadn't been made. But mistakes are made and accidents happen. The girl and the grandmother learned from both. The dog recovered. He even learned to run again." Grandma smiled.

"But it was my fault!" Erin could feel the tears snake down her cheeks. "My fault," she repeated. "I didn't ask for your permission. And I rushed out of the house without thinking about the springer and the harness. You didn't make the mistake. I did."

Grandma pulled Erin into her arms. "But I could have m'darlin.' Easily. The truth is I never would have bought the springer. Never. It didn't occur to me until John showed up with it. I would have let you ride with Blue just like you did last year."

She wiped her tears away. "You're just saying that to make me feel better."

"No, I'm not." Grandma pulled back and looked into Erin's eyes. Her gaze was steady, open. "Honest."

Erin frowned. "You said there was more traffic around here."

"Yes," the older woman agreed, "there is. But it's not something I think about every day. Now you listen to me, Erin Morris. What's over is over. I feel terrible about Blue. I do. And I know you do, too. But we have to move forward. I will not have you feeling guilty about what happened. Yes, you could have remembered the harness and springer. But the fact is, if it had been left up to me, you wouldn't have had that springer at all."

"Oh, Grandma." Erin began to sob. "I'm so sorry. I just wish it hadn't happened."

Grandma's arms went around her again. Soothingly she rubbed Erin's back. "I know what you wish, m'darlin'. But what's done is done. Don't look back. Look forward. Think of the future."

After a few minutes, her sobs turned to sniffles. Forward. Going home. Back to school. Leaving Blue.

Grandma pulled her up. "There's something I

want you to do for me," she said, as they walked toward the house.

"What's that?" Erin asked.

"You haven't seen Blue since the accident. Your mom offered to take you a couple of times and you refused. I know it's a difficult thing to do, but I want you to go and see him. He's sad, Erin. Maybe you can cheer him up."

"Me?" She practically choked on the word. How could she do anything for Blue? She'd already ruined his life. There was nothing left to do.

"Yes," Grandma said, holding open the back door. "You. If you won't do it for me, do it for Blue."

———————————— ·⊂⊃

Erin smelled the animal hospital even before she walked through the door. It made her dizzy. Cassie gave her a good-natured shove forward. "Hurry up," she said. "Your grandma's waiting."

Grandma was ahead, speaking to a woman behind a tall white counter. Erin looked over her shoulder, past Cassie, to her grandmother's car parked in the sun. If she could have her way she'd turn around, get into the car, and drive back to Dove Creek Kennels herself. Even though she couldn't drive. "This is a dumb idea," she whispered again to Cassie. "I don't want to be here."

"Your grandma wants you to." Cassie sat on the edge of one of the hard wooden chairs. "Besides, like I told you on the phone last night, if you're going to work at the SPCA when you get home, you'd better get used to sick animals."

"You told me that this morning, too," Erin muttered crossly as she slid into the chair beside Cassie.

"It's true."

Erin glared at her. Sometimes Cassie's mouth was too big for her body. "You're supposed to be making me feel better, not worse!" She looked around the waiting room—at the dog magazines on the table and the pictures on the wall. There was a poster with an old English sheepdog. Its tongue was hanging out and it had a red ribbon around its neck. Kiss Me Quick, the caption read. A second picture showed a mother cat with a group of kittens curled up beside her. It reminded Erin of Duchess and her puppies.

It reminded her of Twister.

This was the place they'd brought Twister to be put to sleep. The same day Blue had been hit by that car. The same day he'd lost his leg. She plugged her nose and tried not to breathe. "It stinks in here," she said to Cassie.

"You're just nervous," Cassie replied matter-of-factly.

"Shut up." With her finger on her nose, the words came out in a squeak.

Cassie sniffed. "I'm going to pretend I didn't hear that," she said.

"Okay, girls." Grandma motioned them forward. "We can go in now."

Cassie stood. Panic seized Erin. She couldn't move. She didn't want to see Blue. She didn't want to see what she'd done to him. She shook her head no.

Cassie leaned close. "It's more scary thinking about it than doing it. My mom told me that, and I hate to admit it but she was right." She pulled on Erin's elbow. "Come on," she said again.

Grandma gave her an encouraging smile. "Dr. Maartens is waiting for us."

It felt like forever before Erin could force her legs to work. Finally she stood up.

The woman came out from behind the counter. She led them through a door and down a hallway. The horrible hospital disinfectant smell grew stronger. Erin felt light-headed. Her legs wobbled like they did when she'd been sick for a long time.

Click, click, click. Their feet echoed off the walls. A dog barked in the distance; a man laughed. The woman stopped in front of a door that said Recovery.

"Dr. Maartens is already with him," she told Grandma with a smile. She opened the door and Grandma stepped through.

Cassie looked at Erin. Erin looked at Cassie.

Go, Cassie mouthed silently.

Erin swallowed the sour taste of fear that tickled the back of her throat. She went.

The recovery room was a long, skinny space like her grandmother's kennel. Running along one side was a series of cages—little rooms, really—with metal bars that ran from floor to ceiling. On the other side were cupboards and a sink. Soft music played from an unseen radio. Slowly, slowly, Erin followed her grandmother past empty cages to one near the end.

"Hello, Dr. Maartens," Grandma said as she came to a stop. "How's Blue today?"

"About the same as yesterday," a voice replied. "Still a little too quiet for my liking."

Erin stopped suddenly and Cassie smashed into her back. Dr. Maartens was in the cage. So was Blue.

"*Go*," Cassie hissed.

She edged forward. Nervously she looked between the metal bars into the cage. Blue was asleep on his side. He had a large, white bandage wrapped around one foreleg. Dr. Maartens was crouched beside him—a heavy-set man wearing khakis and a yellow sweater.

Erin stared at Blue. For a minute she thought they'd made a mistake. That he still had his other leg. But then she realized all that white was just a whole lot of bandage. With no leg inside. She felt dizzy again. Quickly she looked away.

"Hello, Erin," Dr. Maartens said gently. His blue eyes were kind above his bushy gray moustache. "This must be very hard for you."

Tears gathered and stung. She opened her mouth to speak but she couldn't. The sour taste of fear was back, and it was the size of a jawbreaker in her throat.

"She's very brave." Grandma gave her an encouraging smile.

Cassie jabbed her in the side. "Say something," she urged under her breath. "Talk to him. To Blue."

But Erin couldn't say a word. Dr. Maartens understood. "He's going to be fine, Erin," he assured her. "Even without his front leg. Blue's going to make it."

She nodded. Involuntarily her eyes were drawn back to Blue. The dog was stirring. "Hello, Blue," she whispered. "Hello, my darling Mr. Lavender Blue."

The dog sprang to life. He stood and tried to rush

to the front of the cage. To Erin. With a whimper he crashed back to the ground. His tail thumped against the floor and he tried to pull himself forward, whimpering all the while.

Erin didn't know whether to laugh or cry. And so she did both. Dr. Maartens chuckled and stood up. "That's the most excitement I've seen out of him since he got here." He opened the door of the cage and motioned her inside. "Come on in," he said. "Somebody wants to say hi to you."

She hesitated. What if she touched his bandage? What if she hurt him all over again?

"It's okay." Dr. Maartens seemed to know what she was thinking. He shut the cage behind her. "Just kneel in front of him."

Erin tried. But before her knees touched the ground, Blue edged forward and lunged. He was all over her. His tongue kissed her cheeks, her ears, her jaw. His nose traveled back and forth across her face, through her hair, around her neck.

She steadied herself and threw her arms around him. "Hello, Blue, my Lavender Blue." She buried her face in his fur and let the tears fall again. "I'm so sorry, Blue. It's all my fault. I'm so sorry I—"

But Blue wouldn't let her finish. He began another enthusiastic round of kissing. He still whimpered with excitement; his tail still *thump, thumped* madly against the floor.

"This is good to see!" Dr. Maartens grinned. "Blue was improving physically but he hasn't been a very happy dog."

"Erin has always been his favorite," Grandma said. She and Cassie watched from outside the cage. "Even when he was a small puppy. I was hoping her visit would cheer him up."

"It certainly has." Dr. Maartens said.

But Erin's heart was breaking. With every kiss and every whimper she was reminded all over again of what she'd done to Blue. It was all her fault he'd lost a leg. All her fault he'd never win another dog show.

"Blue needs a lot of love and attention," Dr. Maartens said when Blue was finally finished his kissing spree. "He's going to have to learn to walk and run all over again."

The dog's head rested on Erin's knee; his eyes were dark and loving as they stared up at her. Every once in a while, when Erin looked back at him, his tail would thump against the floor.

God had answered her prayers, Erin reminded herself as she scratched Blue in that soft spot behind his ears. Half-answered them at least. Blue was okay.

He hadn't died. But he wasn't full of spit and vinegar like he used to be. And he never would be.

"It's going to take a special person," Dr. Maartens was saying. "Someone with a lot of time and patience to work with him."

"I think we can arrange that," Grandma said.

Something in her grandmother's voice made Erin look up. Grandma was smiling. Cassie was smiling. Dr. Maartens was smiling.

"Pardon?" Erin frowned. She must have missed something.

"You wanted a dog, m' darlin'. And Blue's going to need a very special home. He's going to need what you were going to give to Twister. How about it, Erin?" Grandma raised her eyebrows. "How about taking Blue home with you?"

A three-legged dog? Her three-legged dog.

"No!" The answer was out of her mouth before she had time to think about it. "I...I...I can't do that." She jumped up. Blue whined at her sudden movement. "Come on, Cassie." She wouldn't look at Dr. Maartens or her grandmother. "Let's wait in the car."

Erin played with her French fries, dipping them into the pool of vinegar on her plate and then into the little mound of salt. She'd been happy when her mother had suggested lunch at Mudsharks Coffee Bar, but after the drive into downtown Courtenay and getting a seat on the terrace overlooking Fifth Street, her appetite had disappeared.

"You all packed?" Mom bit into a lettuce leaf.

Erin nodded. Dip, dip. Roll in salt. Dip again. "This summer has gone so fast." She sighed. Blue was home now, recuperating nicely, though he was still quiet at times, and not as energetic as Erin would have hoped. Dr. Maartens said to give him more time.

"It's nice that we've had some holiday time together."

Erin nodded a second time. Mom was trying so hard to be supportive. She hadn't even said a thing about the dangers of grease when Erin had ordered a cheeseburger and fries. Listlessly she bit into a French fry. Yuck. Too much salt.

"Don't eat it if you don't want to," Mom said. "This heat is enough to kill anyone's appetite."

"No kidding," Erin muttered. It wouldn't be so bad if she had worn shorts instead of pants this morning. But the hair on her legs was growing back and the self-tanner had faded. She felt self-conscious again. Rotten, irresponsible *and* self-conscious. A triple whammy. If she complained to Mom, she'd probably let her use the self-tanner again. Anything to get her to smile. But who cared? The perfect reinvention just wasn't the same without the perfect Mr. Lavender Blue to go with it. Erin pushed her plate away.

"I understand you have a decision to make," her mother said casually.

She knew exactly what her mother meant. "I've already made it."

Just then the waitress appeared with the bill. "Anything else for you?" she asked.

Mom smiled, shook her head, and handed the waitress a twenty-dollar bill. "Mistakes are funny things," her mother continued when the waitress was gone. "Most of the time you don't know you've made one until they're over. But sometimes you can see them coming." She scraped up the last of the salad on her plate.

Erin frowned. "What do you mean?"

"Blue needs a home." She crunched on a crouton. "Grandma thinks he'd be happiest with you. Your dad and I think she's right."

Erin didn't answer. If she took Blue home, she'd be reminded of the accident every second of every day. Of *her* mistake. After that talk with her grandmother, she didn't feel guilty anymore. But she still felt responsible. After all, the accident *was* her fault. Nothing would change that.

"Here's a chance to right a wrong, Erin," her mother said in a soft voice. "To catch a mistake before it happens."

She watched a group of kids joke and giggle as they sat down at the table next to them. One of the girls had blonde hair just like Rachel. She knew what Rachel would say if she took Blue home.

Her mother followed Erin's eyes. "You're afraid of what the other kids will say, aren't you?"

She shrugged. "No. Yes—I don't know! You should see the way they treat this dog called Patches," Erin said. "It's awful."

"They could learn from you."

"Blue's just not the kind of dog I thought I'd get. He's...he's...he's just not."

Her mother's eyes were thoughtful. "Was Twister?" she asked.

"Twister was beautiful," Erin said hotly. "And he was a little puppy. Nobody makes fun of little puppies. Besides, he had time to grow. Time to become perfect. And he would have been, too."

Mom smiled. "There's no such thing as perfection, sweetheart. We've all got our warts." Her eyes dropped to Erin's left hand. "Even if the real ones disappear, the imperfections are still there." She reached for her water. "Perfection isn't possible."

Her mother was wrong. "Yes, it is." Erin had tasted perfection. In the ring with Blue.

"People aren't perfect," her mother repeated after she put her glass down. "Not Rachel, not me, not you, not your dad." She grinned and Erin could see a sliver of green lettuce stuck between her front teeth. "That's what makes us all so interesting. Same with dogs. They aren't perfect, either. In fact, if you wait for the perfect dog to come along, you'll be waiting forever."

Erin picked up her lemonade and considered Mom's words. Rachel not perfect? Or Mom or Dad, either? Well, Rachel *did* have one eye that was bigger than the other, and she had a horrible temper sometimes. And Dad was impatient and Mom was obsessed with natural everything.

But what about the perfect reinvention? Well, even with all that hard work, Erin had to admit she was still clumsy and too tall—and she daydreamed way too much. Not only that, if she was honest about it, the dog show hadn't been perfect either. Sure, she and Blue had won. But she had tripped over that rock and Blue had almost refused to open his mouth and she'd practically missed that trick question about the breastbone.

If there wasn't any such thing as perfection then what had she tasted in the ring? Maybe the purest form of happiness it was possible to taste.

"Think about taking Blue home," Mom suggested. "Okay?"

"I'll think about it," Erin finally said. "But I'm not planning on changing my mind." A three-legged dog was worse than a bald and smelly one. She'd never live it down. And she'd never forget her mistake, either.

"Your dad and I love you, no matter what," her mother said, wiping her fingers on a napkin and pushing her plate away. "Don't you think Blue deserves the same thing?"

Epilogue

"**I** GOTTA GO, RACHE." Erin tried, for the third time, to get off the phone with her friend. She had only twenty minutes until Dan would be by to lock up for the night, and there was still a lot to do.

"Then promise you'll come to the party with me?" Rachel begged on the other end of the line. "You gotta show off your cool new haircut and that great Gap sweater. Besides, the Oresti twins will be there, and I think Zach Cameron will be, too," she added slyly.

Erin flushed at the mention of Zach's name. "I'll see," she said firmly. "Now I've got to go!" She hung up and turned back to the SPCA sponsor list on the desk in front of her. Same old Rachel. Still fixated on boys and clothes and looks.

Erin liked to look good, too, but right now she was more concerned with finishing the address list before she went home. Volunteering for the occasional night shift had its advantages. It was a lot

250

quieter than working a weekend. She could get more done.

She picked up her pen and began to write. A whimper from Blue stopped her. She looked up, her heart pounding the way it always did when Blue cried. The dog slept in his favorite corner in the waiting room. His eyelids twitched, his tail swished softly on the brown carpet. He whimpered again. Erin smiled. He was just dreaming.

Her heart slowed but she kept her eye on him. Unbelievable that she'd almost left him in Courtenay because she was so worried about what other people would think of a three-legged dog.

Zach Cameron seemed to think Blue was just fine. And, as far as boys went, Zach was fine, too. For one thing, he had a dog. A spunky Irish Setter named Lucille. They sometimes bumped into each other walking their dogs on Grand Boulevard. Blue seemed to have a thing for redheads and Erin could tell Lucille had the hots for Blue. For another thing, Zach was taller than her, which meant she didn't have to look down when they talked, and he was gently playful with Blue, which she appreciated.

Erin returned to her list. The T's were done. No sponsors under U. Just a few under V and W, and then she'd be finished. If she kept taking on extra work and extra shifts, Dan was sure to give her a paying job. Erin really wanted a paying job. She could see it now.

She would buy a second Retriever. A yellow Lab this time. She'd call her Lilith, or maybe Genevieve. Blue would be the dad and the new dog would have puppies. Lots and lots of puppies. Erin would go up and down Lonsdale putting up signs advertising the litter. Zach would help her. She wouldn't let the puppies go to just any—

"Excuse me."

Startled, she looked up. She hadn't heard the door open. Even Blue was still sleeping.

"Sorry if I scared you." A tall, silver-haired man smiled apologetically. "I'm looking for my cat. He's been missing for three days."

Erin gave him a sympathetic smile back. "Let me get the new arrivals list." She grabbed the clipboard that hung on the wall behind her.

The door behind her flew open again. This time she heard it. So did Blue. He woke up with a *woof*.

"Here are your keys, Pops." There was a jingle of metal being tossed.

That voice. She would know it anywhere.

Clipboard in hand, she slowly turned around. Deryk Latham. Wearing his black leather jacket and standing beside the man who was obviously his father.

"H'lo," he said, meeting her eyes once and then quickly looking away. He shifted awkwardly from one foot to the other.

Erin gave him one of those I-really-should-be-nice-so-I-will smiles. "Hello, Deryk," she said politely. He hadn't called her Beast once this year. The perfect reinvention had obviously changed his opinion about her. How silly. She was the very same person. Deryk was the same person, too. He still had that mean, spiteful look in his eyes, and he was still loud and annoying at school.

Blue hobbled over and nudged Deryk's hand. Deryk didn't look down but he did reach out and give him a scratch on the head. "My dad's lost his cat," he said, still moving uncomfortably on his feet.

"What does the cat look like?"

"Long-haired calico. Brown and white, with some orange," Mr. Latham responded. "Wears a bright green collar. Answers to Max. Has a chunk missing out of his right ear."

"We have raccoons near our place." Deryk's laugh sounded nervous. He ran a hand through his hair. "He probably got in a fight with one." Blue licked his hand. This time Deryk glanced down.

Did he see Blue's missing leg? She couldn't tell. "When did the cat disappear?" she asked.

"Halloween night," Mr. Latham said. "He hates loud noises."

She scanned back to October 31. Nothing. "I know we have a calico cat with a missing ear in one of the cages," she murmured, looking at the intake for November 1. "A male, too, I think. There he is. A brown and white long-haired." She read from Dan's notes. "Possible calico. Wearing a green collar. Looks well-cared for. Missing part of his right ear." Erin looked up and grinned. "Sounds like Max."

Mr. Latham looked relieved. So did Deryk.

"Come on." She put the clipboard back on its hook. "I'll take you back to him." She walked out from behind the desk. "Let's go, Blue." The black Retriever hobbled to Erin's side.

Deryk's eyes widened. "*That's* Blue?" He stared at the empty place where Blue's right front leg should have been. "The champion you've been talking about?"

"That's him, all right." Erin pulled herself up and looked Deryk Latham straight in the eye. "And he is a champion." She grinned. "*My* champion. Now let's get Max." She turned toward the kennel door.

"*Woof!*" Blue nudged her hand.

She laughed and gave him a playful tug on the ear. "He doesn't like to be left behind," she explained to Deryk and his father. She looked down into Blue's warm, dark eyes. They held so much love—love she had almost turned away from. "Okay, Blue," Erin said softly. "Go ahead."

With his head up and tail held high, Mr. Lavender Blue proudly led the way through the doors and back to the cage that held Max the calico cat.